CITY OF NIGHT
BOOK I

AURORA GREY

CITY OF NIGHT

THE TAVERN
AT THE END
OF THE WORLD

N

BOOKS BY AURORA GREY

The City of Night Series

(A Crowns of Aureon Series)

City of Night

Song of Night

The Dark Fae Guardian Series

(A Crowns of Aureon Series)

House of Gilded Nightmares

Court of Bone and Amethyst

Lord of Broken Memories

The Raven Society Series

Hot Hex

Hex on the Beach

Hex in the Highlands

Viking Hex

Revenge Hex

www.auroragreyauthor.com

To all my fellow witches and romantasy lovers
who feel the stir of magic in their souls

CHAPTER
ONE
ZARA

F rom the shadows of the bell tower, I watch the glittering lights and sparkling gowns of the crowd far below. The beauty and finery strike a harsh contrast to the truth of this place, a thin veneer over the darkness that lives here, the black heart of the City of Night.

They've gathered to pay their respects to the one who rules it all. The one who controls the wild magic, who keeps us living in fear day in and day out. A hated and reviled leader, the devil watching over our Hell. The Lord of Night.

No one hates him more than I do.

Which is why I plan to kill him.

A cold wind whips around the tower as if trying to pry me from my hiding place. The enormous bell is close enough to touch on my left, and where my arm wraps around one of the slender columns supporting the roof, the

1

coolness of the stone kisses my skin. I can feel the magic in the stone as well. It runs through this city like blood, the arteries that keep life pumping through it. An ancient magic that lived here long before these walls went up.

The wind reminds me it's time to move, I have work to do tonight. Stepping into the moonlight, I jump from the tower onto the battlement twenty feet below, landing lightly on the soles of my boots. I'm dressed entirely in black, both form-fitting pants and a jacket made from silk and leather. I don't need dark clothing to blend into the night, but it's become a bit of a habit. I am a product of this city, through and through. Night and shadow and magic.

From the top of the battlement, I'm still high enough to see the vast city sprawling below me. The river is a black shimmer to the north, a line which cannot be crossed unless one wishes a swift and painful death. That's if you're lucky, and it's not a slow and agonizing death after weeks of torture. House Angelus does not take kindly to trespassers. The river itself belongs to House Syreni, and the southern part of Night is occupied by House Daemonium and House Animus.

I used to dream of life on the north side of the river. As a child, I figured it must be better there. I'd sneak away and sit by the water, staring across to the distant shore, a mere couple hundred feet separating me from happiness. The Syreni, or the Mer as most people call them, would swim to the riverbank and sing about the beautiful life that awaited me if I crossed to the other side. Such gorgeous creatures, large eyes and bright hair, it was hard to believe they wished me harm. I'd nearly obeyed them one day, before my sister Jaylen yanked me back from the edge as those alluring faces attempted to snatch me beneath the surface.

That was the day I learned there isn't a good part of this city. We're all mired in the same darkness.

I shake my head to bring me back to the task at hand. My feet carry me across the stones to a set of steps leading down to the streets below. I have to be careful—I'm in Daemonium territory now, far from the relative safety of my home in the Animus sector several miles to the east. All four of the great houses are ruled by the Lord of Night, but only by the thinnest of truces, an agreement more fragile than the finest ceramic teacup. Which is one of the reasons the event going on in the courtyard below is such a farce. The annual allegiance ball, where all the factions get together to renew their loyalty. It's a night that will most definitely end in bloodshed. And some display of magic by the Lord to instill terror in his citizens, the reason, no doubt, he's maintained control of Night for so long.

Which is exactly why I've come.

To see if *this* night, someone will take him down. And to ensure, if they do not, that I finish the job.

I pause when I reach the base of the steps, centering myself before moving away from the shelter of the building. Taking in a breath, I force my heart to still its racing, force the adrenaline to calm in my veins. I've waited a decade for this night. Since the day the Lord of Night took the thing most important to me. I must maintain focus. I've waited too long for this.

On my next breath, I call to the shadows. A summoning of wild magic and the night surrounding me, both of which eagerly respond. Most never notice me even when I'm not cloaked by darkness, because even without magic I've become very good at blending in. But once the shadows wrap around me I'm completely invisible, even to the most observant of gazes. There are few who can wield the shadows as I can, because it calls for a control over the wild magic most do not possess. Calling on the magic is a roll of the dice each time. The magic may yield to you, or it may consume you.

In this war-torn city, many rely on it to survive, but it takes its payment in souls.

I stride for the courtyard, my long hair whipping out behind me in the wind. Within a few moments, I've passed between the row of guards checking invites at the gates of the Palace of Night. One of them turns his head slightly, nostrils flared as I slide past, no doubt feeling the breeze of my passing or catching my scent for a moment. But he shakes his head a moment later and turns his attention to the street once again, clearly dismissing the sensation.

Turning, I skirt the edge of the courtyard. I can't have any of the Animus sniffing me out, as their sense of smell is vastly superior to that of the Daemonium palace guard. I may live among the Animus, but I'm not one of them. And there is one in particular I cannot allow to see me tonight.

My eyes wander over the crowd. I watch people in fine

clothes, eating luxurious food and sipping sparkling golden wine the likes of which my lips have never tasted. Towering cascades of flowers dot the tiled courtyard, and musicians strum gilded instruments that color the air with song. Teeth flash as lips part in smiles, and bubbles of laughter ripple throughout.

None of that, however, can cover the thick tension that hangs in the ether, strung tighter than a hundred crossbows at the ready. Each person here is prepared to kill their neighbor at the slightest provocation. Many are already planning it, even now as they smile and sip their wine.

I don't know of a time when the four great houses were not at war. And I don't think anyone else remembers such a time, either. It's always been this way. This eternal battle for control of the city and the magic at its heart. Generation after generation born into it, none of us knowing exactly why it started, just that we belong to it.

Belong to *him*.

They're all here: Animus and Syreni, Angelus and Daemonium. And, of course, the ones like me, who can wield the wild magic without any innate magic of their own. The Incantrix. The ones who belong to no particular house, who belong to everyone and to no one.

The Daemonium vastly outnumber the other factions present, as their main goal tonight is to keep control of their power, maintain the seat of Night. The allegiance ball is always held at the home of the reigning ruler, which has been the Daemonium for as long as I've been alive. It's the deadliest night of the year, an event discussed for weeks before and after. And an event I've never attended before, since only the leaders of each house and their top officials are invited.

It's fascinating to see all of them together. The Angelus with their beautiful wings thrumming with magic, feathers of blue or gold or darkest obsidian, or the occasional jade or silver. The Syreni, here by virtue of Incantrix spellwork, floating within orbs of liquid from the waist down so they can leave the river. The Animus, who of course I am most familiar with, looking mostly ordinary but for their eyes, which reveal the beast within, and occasionally another tell-tale feature: golden scales along the cheeks, claws at the ends of their fingers, teeth a bit too sharp to be ordinary.

And then there are the Daemonium. Their appearances range across a broad spectrum. Those who drink blood possess the beauty of the Angelus but without the wings, paired with the predatory grace of the Animus. Those ruled by fire and brimstone have eyes to match, and often horns or leathery wings.

In comparison to the others, the Incantrix are the most ordinary in appearance. Our only tell is our eyes, eyes which glow in varying shades of purple. A faint ring around the pupil marks a novice magic wielder, whereas a full pupil in a richer shade of purple marks a skilled Incantrix. Though not all Incantrix are born with the ability. At the age of ten, we are tested to see if we can summon the wild magic. If we can, we are sent to the leader of our house to serve. And if we are unmagicked, we are sometimes sent anyways, to become housekeepers or cooks or medics.

Because everything in Night, both objects and people, must serve the war.

There is so much magic thrumming through the courtyard, and so many different types of it, that I have to take several deep breaths to regain my focus. I concentrate on the stone tiles beneath my boots, on the cool autumn air sliding over my skin. The Incantrix have the ability to sense the wild magic much more so than the others. That's where we are different. And where I am more different than all the rest.

My focus returns and I continue my journey along the edge of the courtyard. Finally, I turn my gaze to the one I'd come here to see.

He sits in a huge stone chair at the far end of the tiled plaza, hidden mostly in shadow but for two flickering bowls of fire set atop marble pillars on either side of him. He's a good twenty feet beyond the edge of the festivities, alone, without even guards. The Lord of Night needs no one to guard him. No one sane would voluntarily come anywhere within the confines of this courtyard, let alone to stand before him.

Which, of course, begs the question of why I'm foolish enough to be here.

The desire for revenge makes you blind like that.

I've only ever seen him from afar, at least a quarter mile off. He's tall, I can tell even though he's sitting down. His chest and shoulders are broad like a warrior, not that he ever has to get close enough to his victims for hand-to-hand combat. In the shifting light of the torches, I see glimpses of sun-darkened skin, but the top half of his face is covered by a mask made of pewter. In the darkness, I can't tell what color his eyes are. He watches over the crowd with an expression devoid of emotion.

My feet carry me forward, my gut roiling with a twisted obsession to be closer to the one who destroyed my life. The Lord of Night draws me like a magnet. He's been my one purpose, my sole reason for existing the last ten years. My waking thought and the last thing I envision before I go to sleep. I am fixated on the physicality of him, the embodiment of my yearning for revenge for so very long.

When I'm a dozen feet away, I abruptly come to my senses and stop myself from going any closer. I'm so close I can sense his magic, a slow spiral of power crouched within him, blazing like the sun and the moon both. It's the most powerful thing I've ever felt.

As my awareness connects to his magic, the Lord of Night slowly turns his head and looks right at me.

His eyes lock onto mine.

CHAPTER
TWO
ZARA

My body goes still, and I clutch my shadows more tightly around me. The Lord of Night's eyes bore into me, and the enormous quantity of magic churning inside him flares. How can he see me? No one has ever seen through my shadow magic before. Cold terror spikes through my blood.

A hand claps over my mouth from behind and I'm lifted off the ground as if I weigh nothing.

The scream in my throat dies as I'm spun into the darkness of an alcove a dozen feet away, my captor moving with lightning speed. When I'm pressed into a wall, my eyes widen in recognition and my pulse slows. I drop my shield of shadows.

"Do you have a death wish?" Lyri growls, low in her throat. Her yellow panther eyes narrow to angry slits. She moves her gloved hand from my mouth. In the dim light coming from the courtyard, I can see her leather breastplate with the dragon head emblem of the Animus, marking her as one of the warriors.

I know nothing I say right now is going to make my best friend forgive me. For the past decade, ever since I lost my sister, Lyri has been everything to me. She'd taken me under her wing the very first day I arrived from the prison camp.

"How did you find me?" I ask softly.

I don't hear any commotion from the courtyard, and I can no longer feel the swell of magic from the Lord of Night. It seems Lyri found me just in time. Or maybe he hadn't really seen me. A coincidence only.

Lyri snorts. "My animal smelled you the moment you entered the courtyard. I just had to find a moment to break away from Kieran without him noticing." She pins me in her feline gaze, then looks over her shoulder as if the Lord of Animus, our commander, is right behind us. "And now I must return. You will head straight to the cathedral without a backward glance."

"I will *not*." Heat stirs in my belly. "I have waited years for this night."

"Listen carefully." Her words come out rushed, desperate. "We have a plan. If you stay, you're only going to interfere."

When I open my mouth to protest, Lyri covers it with her glove again.

"I need you to trust me, Zara. Trust Kieran." She steps away from me. "I've been missed, no doubt. I must go."

Her eyes plead with me. "Please, Zara." She turns and strides back into the courtyard.

My heart races in my chest as indecision wars within me. If I've gotten Lyri in trouble or compromised their plan, I'm never going to forgive myself. She'd only gotten into the inner circle of Kieran's security guard within the last year, and she'd risked everything just now to protect me. What plan do they have? A plan to kill the Lord of Night? Kieran is my mentor, too, the one who trained me all these years in magic and battle skills both. A pang of jealousy moves through me. Why hadn't he trusted me with this?

But Lyri's worried expression still hangs in my mind, and I let out a sigh. I wouldn't abandon my mission for anyone else, but Lyri is like a sister. I would do anything for her. Anything at all.

Decision made, I walk swiftly down the side of the courtyard for the exit, slipping past the guards again. As soon as I'm out of range of their hearing, I run, back to the staircase and up to the battlement where I'd hidden before. I have to know what happens. Even if my own mission has been aborted.

When I reach the top of the battlement, my eyes dart immediately back down to the courtyard to see what's transpired in the brief passage of time it took me to reach this vantage point. A number of people are fanned out before the Lord of Night, standing a dozen or so feet away. After a moment, I realize it's the rulers of each house:

Ellielle of House Angelus, Octavius of House Syreni, and my own leader, Kieran of House Animus.

Behind them stand their advisors and guards. An ordinary person wouldn't be able to make out the details I can, but bending night and shadows is my primary skill as an Incantrix, so my vision in the dark is enhanced. I search the array of faction representatives, but I don't see Lyri. Adrenaline spikes through my blood. Has she been punished because of me?

There's a scroll rolled out atop a pedestal that's been set before the Lord of Night, and alongside it, a feather pen. Each faction leader is supposed to come forward and sign it, pledging their loyalty to the Lord of Night. It's an antiquated annual tradition that does nothing to pause the constant battle for power within the city. I can't comprehend why they even bother with it when the factions would sooner rip out each other's throats than exhibit any loyalty to one another.

But they approach and sign the scroll one by one. First Octavius, floating in his magical orb of river water, his bottom half a shimmer of dark blue scales, his hair golden. Ellielle is next, with her long ebony hair and silver wings, wings which match the thin coronet worn at her brow. Kieran strides forward last, and it's the moment before he reaches the scroll that the night explodes.

From either side of the courtyard, bolts of magic shoot into the Lord of Night. There are at least six assailants, I count that many magical signatures as I watch, the breath leaving my lungs, my heart pounding like an elephant in my ribcage. I lean forward over the battlement, the cool night air rushing around me, my balance almost tipping in the swirl of adrenaline and magic buzzing through my veins.

The Lord of Night stands up from his chair, and even at this distance, I feel the storm of magic he summons.

That's when a giant black panther appears out of the darkness behind him, leaping from the shadows, tackling him to the floor of the courtyard. I would know that feline anywhere, the yellow of those eyes, like burning moons.

Lyri.

I have only a moment to feel the full swell of horror within me before the Lord of Night flings Lyri off of him as if she were nothing but a fly. He stands over her for one long moment, barely flinching as magic continues to pour into him from the Incantrix hidden on each side of the courtyard.

And then his power pulses across Night, a quake moving through the stone buildings. I nearly topple over the edge as the battlement shudders beneath me. He raises one hand and curls his fingers into a fist, ripping the life force out of Lyri and his other attackers. A scream rips from my throat as the glow of their magic and their spirits pours into him. Several Incantrix at the perimeter of the courtyard fall dead and the other guests scatter, bolting for the exits as the Daemonium rush to their leader's aid.

Agony burns through me as I sink to my knees along the battlement wall.

Lyri is gone.

Lyri is gone.

It loops on repeat through my head as I sit against the stone, a fine tremor running through my body. I'm not a stranger to loss, but the impossibility of this, the denial, spins me around like a cyclone.

The night has always been full of color, the shadows nuanced, a palette of midnight hues. But now a blackness falls around me, flat and heavy, cold and silent. I let Lyri convince me to leave, and now she's dead.

Why did I let this happen?

The next few hours pass in a blur. After a time, I extricate myself from the battlement, and somehow, I manage to make my way several miles east back into the Animus sector. Autumn leaves stir in the trees along the streets and in the graveyards I pass. Down an alleyway, I catch the glow of a fire where several residents are huddled, burning an offering to the dark goddess, the one said to watch over the city.

My head is so muddled that I don't hear the sound of footsteps behind me until it's almost too late.

I spin and duck as my assailant lunges past me, the crude wooden club in his hand hitting the side of a building instead. I must have dropped my cloak of shadows without realizing it. A string of curses and a growl roll off my tongue.

The man turns, his face scrunched in anger. Two more step out from the shadows of an abandoned building ahead. Even in my own sector, I must be careful walking alone at night. Everyone wants an Incantrix, since we're the only ones who can make the wild magic obey. The only ones who can rule it instead of being ruled *by* it, especially the Animus, who must turn at the full moon. Or the unmagicked, like these men, who have neither beast nor power.

"You've got a foul mouth," my attacker snarls, twirling his club menacingly.

I cock my head to the side, happy for a distraction from my grief. Sparks of violet light pulse at my fingertips as magic moves through me. "Oh, my language is the problem here, is it?"

"Shut up, *witch*," hisses one of the club-wielder's friends.

The three of them advance on me all at once.

I don't cloak myself in shadows, and I don't handle them as quickly as I could. I want them to see me coming, and I want to take my time with this.

My fingers find my silver daggers, one in my boot, one in my thigh sheath. I crouch as they stumble forward. When they're nearly upon me I spin, darting in and out, my knife taking blood payment from each of them. A chorus of cries and groans rise into the air as I pass, fast as a serpent. They look around in confusion, clutching their injuries as they turn to find I'm now behind them.

Smarter men would run at this point.

They come at me again, trying to be fast this time, rushing me with all the elegance of a trio of circus clowns. I cyclone around them again, taking two bites of my blade from each. One of them falls to his knees, his fingers dark with blood as he holds his puncture wound, and one staggers into a nearby alley. But my original attacker roars and runs toward me like a bull.

The wild magic of Night surges into me without summons, a crackle of violet light surging from my fingers into my would-be abductor. He convulses as the power hits him, eyes rolling back in his head before he falls with a loud thud to the cobblestone street.

I shove down the magic, shaking my hand to dissipate the energy running through me. It feels like I've swallowed a storm. My eyes rove over the man on the ground; he's still breathing, though it's quite shallow. Hopefully when he comes to, he'll think twice about attacking another Incantrix. A tired sigh issues from my lips. It's not the first time, and it certainly won't be the last. In this place, magic is currency, and magic is the difference between life and death.

There will never be a time when I'm safe within Night.

I continue on my way. When the cathedral looms ahead, I skirt the ornate front doors, around back where the clergy used to live. Most of the churches are abandoned and turned into residences like this one. I do not know what deities they worshipped. We know only one lord now, and the dark goddess who is merely a comfort to the citizens of Night. I sometimes wonder what it was like before, and what it's like beyond the city. But I've never traveled outside its borders. None of us have. When the wild magic consumed this place, it cut us off from everything that lay beyond, leaving untraversable wastelands in all directions.

There could be others out there. Or it may be nothing, from horizon to horizon.

Often, it seems I hear those voices from the past when I walk these halls, but tonight my grief muffles their whispers. My legs feel leaden as I climb the stairs to my third-floor quarters, furthest from the main cathedral. I stumble through the door to my room, my heart dropping out of my chest when I see Lyri's bed next to mine.

It's not empty.

Daggers are in my hand before my eyes take in what I'm seeing, *who* I'm seeing. But when he stands, eyes glittering in the dark, my breath leaves my chest in an enormous rush.

"Kieran." I bow, shaking, hurriedly tucking my knives away. "I didn't know it was you."

He stands there a moment in silence as I maintain my bow at the waist. I hear him walk slowly toward me. I try to calm the racing of my heart, but when his fingers touch my chin, my adrenaline spikes and I shiver. He lifts my gaze to his.

"No need for formalities, Zara. Not tonight."

His thumb grazes down my throat as he lowers his hand from my face. Golden eyes burn into mine, and I can feel the stir of the dragon within him. Though I am not considered short, especially for a woman, he towers over me. His long black cloak swirls against my leg as he circles me.

I force my breathing to slow. Why is he here? I didn't even know he knew where my room was. I've trained with him nearly every day for the last decade, but our relationship has always been strictly that: mentor and pupil. Commander and warrior. Even if, over the years, my heart has yearned for something more.

"You were there tonight," he finally says, and his voice is deep and soft like the night. But it does not comfort me.

I know I should be afraid, because what I've done, infiltrating the allegiance ball without his permission, deserves the gravest of punishments. But my anguish over Lyri masks my fear. "Yes."

"Why?" His tone tightens, laced with a threat.

A dragon can always sense a lie. And if I speak falsely to him, I'll only prolong my suffering. I take a deep breath, let it back out slowly. "You know why, Kieran. I want him *dead*."

He pivots, having completed his circle around me, and his eyes fix on mine once again. "Yes, your desire for vengeance. Because he killed your sister."

"And because Night has suffered under his rule long enough."

He watches me as if he's reading my soul. His eyes rove over my face, and mine over his. Every battle scar, most prominently the one over his left eye. The golden stubble of his beard. Curls shorn short around his head, skin a deep golden-brown from his hours on the practice field, training the warriors.

His lips stretch into a scowl. "I have not mentored you for the last decade, not spent countless hours of my life nurturing your magic, all for you to throw your life away recklessly, Zara."

"I would rather it have been me than Lyri," I gasp, my emotions breaking loose within me.

Magic surges as my control slips, and his eyes widen. A lavender aura radiates around my body and the stone walls of the room shake. Kieran's dragon rumbles in his chest at the perceived threat, and his eyes flash a darker gold. He places his huge hands around my biceps, but he does not crush me, which he could, easily.

"Breathe, Zara," he commands. "Don't let your magic get the best of you."

It's something he's said a thousand times during our training sessions. For magical drills, we've always trained away from the other Incantrix, private sessions just the two of us. *Your magic is too strong for the others*, he'd told me after I'd arrived from the prison camp.

I close my eyes and do as he says, taking in a deep, shaky breath, then letting it out slowly. My magic fades. "I'm so sorry," I whisper.

"I'm the one who's sorry," he says. "I know Lyri was like family to you."

I draw in another shuddering breath. Kieran's hands are still wrapped around my arms, and he squeezes gently before sliding them back down. "We will fix this. I promise."

"How?"

"We'll discuss it soon. But not tonight." He raises one

hand and runs a finger along my cheekbone. "Tonight, you need to rest."

We stare at each other for several long moments. *How are we going to fix this? How can we possibly make it right?* My despair threatens to pull me under as a dozen questions battle in my head.

And then Kieran is gone, striding off into the night.

CHAPTER
THREE
ZARA

I t was bad luck that landed us in the prison camp, my sister and me. Our parents were Factionless, ones who swear no allegiance to any of the four houses. They died when I was ten, and we lived on the street for a while before being taken in by some of the other rebels. When they were caught by Daemonium one day, we got drug in along with them and thrown behind bars with the other criminals and deserters of Night.

The past loops on repeat in my head after Kieran leaves. Because if it hadn't been for the prison camp, I might never have met Lyri. And that day is seared in my memory forever.

I was fourteen and my sister twelve. We'd been in the camp three years, being used for our magic to make weapons for the Lord of Night. Each day passed like the one before, about fourteen hours of work followed by dinner and an hour or so of leisure time before bed in our cells.

Until one day it didn't.

Daemonium had come for the Incantrix who lived in the prison camp, to take any who could wield magic to the Palace of Night. They'd taken every single one of them, except me, because I'd been in a supply closet when they came. I'd hidden when I heard the commotion, unsure what was happening, and by the time I figured it out, they'd taken my sister.

I walked out of the prison that day, turning myself into pure shadow and moving through the walls. I'd never tested the limits of my magic until that moment of panic. It was then I realized I was special, even among the Incantrix. Because when I called on my magic that day, I *felt* Night, felt the wild magic as it if spoke to me, a soft voice in my head.

After escaping, I made my way to the Palace of Night to rescue my sister. Or tried to, but along the way I got caught. Lyri found me and saved me from walking into the literal devil's den. Naturally, I'd rewarded her by punching her in the face with a fistful of magic. When I came to after she choked me out, I was at the castle of the Animus with all the warriors.

From that day forward, everything changed. I'd wanted, of course, to go back immediately to rescue my sister. But Kieran insisted, rightfully so, that I wasn't ready yet to face the Lord of Night. He began training with me

22

every day. I hadn't known my sister would die before I had the chance to set things right.

Lyri had been there for me that day, too, a couple months after my arrival, when Kieran told me one of his spies caught wind of her murder. Struck down by the Lord of Night in some random fit of rage for disobedience. My purpose that day changed from rescue to vengeance.

As my bedroom fades from black to the plum-toned hues of dawn, I realize I've been awake all night, thinking of the past. Or perhaps I'd slept, and my dreams had been as vivid as my memories. I can't really tell for sure. All I know is that I still feel numb.

I get up and head to the kitchen in the adjacent building. The sky is gray and pale, as it always is with the fog of the Waste surrounding the city and blocking much of the sunlight. The Animus occupy the cathedral, the castle, and most of the surrounding buildings, a complex around a central courtyard. There's a dining hall, but I usually eat by myself. And today, of all days, I have no desire to see anyone. Well, almost anyone.

As I cross the courtyard I scan for Kieran. His words from the night before ring in my head. *We will fix this. I promise.* What is he planning? The need-to-know burns like a thousand torches in my chest, in the pit of my stomach. Now I have not one life to avenge, but two. Every minute that passes while the Lord of Night still breathes is a minute too long.

I will *end* him.

Everything in my life has led to this one goal. Kieran

always knew I was special. He'd said it from the first moment he'd laid eyes on me. He'd trained me himself, something he didn't do with any other Incantrix, which is why I've lived the last decade ostracized by my own kind. Always the teacher's pet, the envied one. I've given everything toward this one purpose.

Why hadn't he chosen me instead of Lyri?

After all these years of training, I'm finally ready to confront the Lord of Night. I need Kieran to see that.

I catch only a glimpse of him on the far side of the courtyard, but he's surrounded by his warriors, so I don't approach. Instead, I hurry on to the kitchen. I can feel his eyes follow me; he's always had the uncanny ability to sense when I'm nearby.

After I eat a quick meal of bread and cheese, I wander about the complex, trying to find out what's going on. I wrap shadows around me, moving unseen in the early morning, catching snippets of conversation. The warriors, Animus and Incantrix both, are preparing for a counterstrike from the Daemonium. Scouts and spies have been sent out across the sector to watch for movement from the enemy. That's usually my job, and something I would have been tasked with, no doubt, had Kieran not been allowing me time to grieve. I also hear discussion of Lyri's funeral. It will take place at sunset, provided we aren't under attack.

As soon as I find out what I need to know, I leave the castle complex. I have too much energy and emotion running through me to stay here and wait. For the attack.

For the funeral. For my chance to get revenge. It feels like I'm slowly burning alive from the inside out. As if the wild magic that moves through me each day has finally gotten the upper hand.

I certainly wouldn't be the first resident of Night to die that way. I probably wouldn't even be the first one this week.

Morning fades to afternoon as I skirt the Daemonium sector, then move north along the river and Syreni territory. I pick up a good bit of intel from both factions, nothing terribly surprising, but info I'll share with Kieran later. As I travel along the water, I catch sight of the tall towers in Angelus territory, both stone and metal. I've often wondered if they build them so high to try and see beyond the Waste, or if it's merely an affinity for the sky. You'd think they could fly beyond this place, or that the Syreni could swim up the river and escape Night. But the magical damage of the Waste stretches to the heavens it seems, and poisons the water within its borders. None who have attempted to pass through it, by land, sky, or water, have made it back to tell the tale.

By late afternoon I've returned to my own sector. Without meaning to, I find myself in one of the many cathedrals near our complex, the place where I practice my magic. I need to lose myself in something now, to forget about Lyri and my sister. I stand in the middle of the cavernous structure watching the pattern of rainbow colors cast by a rare beam of sunlight through the stained-glass windows. Then, I close my eyes.

Magic hums in my veins. It's always there, waiting for me to turn my attention to it, like a starved kitten. Or a starved tiger, rather. It hangs in the air, coming into my lungs with every breath. But more so, I feel it beneath my feet, in the stone, and further down, in the earth beneath the stone. In my mind's eye it's a giant glowing violet force pulsating through everything. A restless dragon crouched beneath the City of Night, waiting to be unleashed.

I've never told anyone I can feel Night in this way, like a living thing. Not even Kieran. Instinctually, I know it makes me even more unique than I already am, beyond my rare shadow magic, because none of the other Incantrix have ever spoken of such a connection to the source of the wild magic. Most have to use spells and words of power to keep it in check, rather than letting it move freely as I can. So, it's a secret I protect fiercely, always holding back, always making sure no one can see my full capabilities.

I'm not even sure *I* truly know.

I let the magic run through me now without much thought or discipline. It's reckless, but I can't bring myself to care. I call to the air and float high above the floor of the cathedral. I call fire and swirl spheres of it between my fingers. I deepen the shadows until it is pitch black within the cathedral and I can't see my own hand in front of my face.

I've seen the remains of Incantrix who lose control of the wild magic. The incinerated bones, sometimes a mere pile of ash. It's a gamble each time we summon power, and even the other creatures of Night can overextend: an Animus who tries to shift outside of the moon cycles, a Daemonium who pushes the limits of their innate power. Sometimes it doesn't bring death, but it takes a vast toll on the body or mind. But with the ongoing war and the effort to survive in this desolate place, everyone takes that risk, day in and day out, never knowing when the magic could turn against them.

When I hear footsteps approaching, I drop the shadows I'd summoned and cast aside my magic. I know who it is, I can sense the power of his inner beast.

"I knew I'd find you here," Kieran says as he approaches.

It's not a leap in logic. We meet here nearly every day. It's *our* place, the place he drills me on my magic, away from the eyes of the other Incantrix.

"I needed to…" I trail off, my throat thickening with tears.

"It seems perhaps you've done enough magic for the day." His golden eyes graze over me. "Have you drilled on anything else?"

I shake my head.

Kieran nods. "Well, then." He bows slightly at the waist, hands fisted at his forehead, and then he attacks.

He doesn't shift into dragon form, though his animal roils just beneath the surface. Heat and raw power and lightning fast, he comes at me with a leap and a round-house kick. I duck and spin beneath the arc of his leg, popping up behind him and throwing a punch. Kieran blocks it easily and makes his own swipe at me.

We continue like this, moving in a blur back and forth across the cathedral floor. I don't use my magic. It's purely physical, muscle and flesh and speed and breath. During one of my rolls across the floor, my hair pops lose from its binding and cascades along my cheek in a wave of ebony. I toss it behind my shoulder, but in that momentary lapse of focus, Kieran lands a kick to my chest.

As I fall backward he follows me, straddling my hips and pinning my arms down. For a moment we're face to face, our breath mingled. His skin is covered in a slight sheen of sweat, and his eyes burn into mine. The roil of feelings in my chest spins in an entirely different direction. Kieran has always been strictly a mentor and a leader. It's a line that can't be crossed. That *shouldn't* be crossed. If he knew how I felt it would ruin everything, and I can't lose the last person that means something to me.

I buck my hips and use the momentum to flip him over. As I land in a straddle over him, a growl pours from his lips and his dragon flashes behind his eyes. Our gazes lock for a moment, and then Kieran stands in one fluid movement, lifting me with him as he goes, as if I weigh nothing.

"Well done," he says, though his tone is deep, almost gruff. "We'd better head back to the complex to get ready."

I blink several times, confused at his sudden shift in mood. Have I offended him somehow? It's not as if this is the first time I've won one of our matches.

"Of course." I give him a sharp nod.

He begins to stride off, but then he turns to face me, so quickly I almost run into him.

"After the funeral, we will discuss what comes next."

This time, when Kieran spins and walks away, he doesn't look back.

CHAPTER

FOUR

KIERAN

L yri's body is laid out across a pyre made of wood that stands in one of the chambers beneath the earth, in the catacombs of old. Torches along the walls chase away the deep shadows, as do the Incantrix, many of whom hold balls of glowing lavender light in their hands. Beyond the murmurs of those who have gathered, I can feel the stir of the spirits that reside here, the magic and hum of centuries past.

I am responsible for the soul that now joins them.

She looks peaceful, the poor girl I sent to her death. Her red hair flames out around her, bright as the torches, and she's been placed in white leather, opposite the dark fittings she wore as my warrior. Her hands are crossed over her chest, a dagger placed between her fingers. I'm relieved we have the body at all. One of my Incantrix summoned it last night amidst the chaos as we escaped the Palace of Night.

It's more than just a casualty of war. Each one of those weighs heavily on me, like iron shackles, and over the last two centuries, I've collected more shackles than I can ever shed.

But Lyri is dead because I did not send someone else.

Because I could not bear to.

My eyes flick across the space to Zara. She's nearly hidden in shadows, standing up against a wall embedded with ancient brown skulls, a sheet of raven hair hiding half her face. I'm not sure she'll ever forgive me. For what I've already done, and for what I must do next.

"We gather tonight to send this brave warrior to the next step of her journey," I call across the room, my voice echoing beneath the earth. "Her spirit travels tonight where we cannot follow."

I pull my eyes from Zara's stoic face and look up at Lyri on the pyre.

"Lyri was a brave warrior who sacrificed her life for our cause. She will be remembered and revered by the Animus until we are no longer." I pull in another breath, feeling the turn of the centuries behind and the centuries ahead. "As earth is the element of our people, so here beneath the surface, in the womb, Lyri shall return."

Others come up and speak after I do, sharing memories and farewells. Zara, though she loved her deeply, more than anyone, does not come forward. She's never been one of many words, nor does she like to be the center of attention.

After everyone has had a chance to speak, those of us

who can shift release our animals, and the Incantrix summon their magic. We growl and howl and sing and shake the catacombs with our voices, sending Lyri's spirit into the next realm, to the mysteries beyond.

When it is done some time later, we climb the stairs beneath the earth until we are above it again. The night air makes me feel exposed as it slices down from above. Exposed and alone, though I'm surrounded by dozens of my warriors. In the moonlight, I search for Zara among the crowd. I catch her scent before I see her, a heady mix of magic and sandalwood. When I turn in the direction of it, I see her standing along one of the walls of the compound. Her purple eyes glimmer for a moment like a cat.

I stride toward her, and when I get close, she separates from the wall and follows me without a word. Across from the cathedral is a small stone tower that stands next to the castle. I push open the wooden door and climb the spiraling stairs. When I reach the top, I catch a glimpse of the city beyond through an open window. It glows like a hoard of gemstones, and the moon illuminates a moss-covered gargoyle perched atop the adjacent parapet.

I push open the door to my chambers and cross the room. Zara's footsteps behind me stop. I turn to see her standing just outside. "Are you going to come in?"

She steps hesitantly inside. "We've never met here before," she says softly, her eyes darting around.

She's right. There's a very specific reason I've never brought Zara to my bedroom before. But I'm too tired tonight to fight myself along with everything else.

I cross to the fireplace and throw a log into it before using a candle and oil to light it. Using the metal poker, I nurture it until the flames take hold and gnaw hungrily at the wood, sending vermillion sparks up the chimney. Finally, I turn back around, and gesture to one of the wing-back chairs in front of it.

"Please, sit."

Zara folds herself gracefully into the chair, as fluid as the shadows she commands. The flames flicker in her eyes.

"I wish we had tonight to grieve," I say, sitting in the chair next to her. "But what comes next requires imme-diate action."

She nods, deadly serious.

"First, I must share with you the plan that failed." I force myself to meet her eyes, even though I hate what I'm about to admit to her. "I had intel that the Incantrix working for the Syreni were planning an attack on the Lord of Night. Which is why I thought Lyri would be able to make her move successfully. While he was distracted."

Zara flinches ever so slightly, no doubt seeing that moment playing out in her head. As I've seen it a thousand times since last night.

"The Lord knows now the Syreni plotted against him. Which is good because he has to split his focus between attacking our two houses. Not to mention, the Angelus are undoubtedly going to plan their own coup while the Lord's forces are occupied. He has to watch his back from every angle."

"This happens after every allegiance ball," Zara says, finally speaking. She keeps her eyes on the fire, avoiding my gaze. "One or more factions make a move to overthrow the Lord, battles ensue. Nothing ever changes."

"It does this time," I say.

My words come out slow, like tar. Zara looks up at me, her eyes bright, expectant.

"I've trained you myself all these years so you could turn the tide, Zara, if it came to that. As a last resort only…"

"A last resort?" Her words lash like a whip. "*Why?* You know I've wanted revenge since nearly the day you took me in. Why did you wait so long? Why…"

She drops off, but we both know what she was going to say. Why did I let Lyri die when I could have sent her sooner?

"I had to be sure you were ready." My eyes burn into hers. "You are so special, Zara. We may never have another shot at this. A chance to end this war once and for all."

"I've been ready," she growls, narrowing her eyes, her gaze shooting like arrows into mine.

"You saw what he did last night." I scowl over at her. "Do not be so cavalier. Even with magic like yours, this will be next to impossible."

"I won't fail," Zara snaps.

"I won't ever forgive myself if you do." I tear my eyes from hers. "Which is why we're going to take a different approach."

She raises her brows, and her lips twitch as if suppressing a retort.

"I am not sending you to assassinate the Lord of Night. Not yet."

"Kieran," Zara begins.

I lift a hand. "You will join his inner circle first, gain his trust."

"How exactly am I supposed to do that?"

"You are an expert spy, you have proven that over the last many years. I am sure you can bring him something— or someone—he will be very grateful to possess."

She sits several moments in silence, clearly digesting my words.

"This might take weeks, or months. But once you've gained his trust, only then will we make our move."

I tap my finger on my thigh, feeling the frenetic energy of my dragon racing through me. It's not just the discussion of enacting a plan nearly ten years in the making. Or the possibility of finally ending this endless war. Being this close to Zara makes my inner beast restless.

"And during your infiltration, you can bring me intel as well, as you always have," I say. "Serve two purposes."

Zara crosses her arms over her chest. "What about the battle ahead? The Daemonium will be attacking soon."

A small smile tugs at my lips. "We can hold our own without you."

She raises her brows again but says nothing.

"You're going to have to keep your desire for revenge at bay, Zara. Don't rush this. But," I pause a moment.

"When the time comes, you're going to need every ounce of your magic. The last decade of discipline has led to this. You're going to want to find someone in the palace to perform your rites with, to keep your power boosted."

Color flushes along Zara's cheeks, making her warm bronze-toned skin even darker. I watch her for a moment, surprised at her shyness. The Animus and Incantrix have long practiced sexual rites, and I know the Daemonium do, too. It's a way to not only share magic, but the resulting climax is often used for certain spells as an energy source. A safer one than summoning the wild magic, and certainly a lot less archaic than the blood sacrifices of centuries past.

A tragic thought crosses my mind. "Oh... was Lyri your..."

Zara shakes her head. She's gone still as stone. "No."

Lyri was the only one Zara got close to. The others were always too jealous of her, because of my special attention and tutoring. If it hasn't been Lyri, then it's likely been no one.

"Is there anything else?" Zara says, her tone reserved, formal almost. "I imagine you want me to leave tonight."

I look at her, realizing the time has finally come for me to let her go. I'd planned this, these many years. I've had plenty of time to come to terms with it. So why is it so difficult?

"Nothing else," I say softly. "Travel well."

CHAPTER
FIVE
ZARA

I get out of my chair and stride for the door. My heart is racing in my chest, adrenaline spiking through my veins. It's finally happening. My plan for revenge is unfolding, even if I do have to play it out longer than I'd like to, as Kieran has instructed. After all these years, I can finally pay that bastard back for what he did to my sister.

Why is it, then, that the forefront of my thoughts is occupied by leaving Kieran? And the embarrassment of him realizing that I haven't been performing my rites like everyone else?

I'd tried years ago to perform rites with one of the Animus warriors, but after we'd begun, I lost control of my magic. It was too strong for him, and I'd hurt him badly. I'd felt so humiliated that day, so horrified. Ever since then, I'd resigned myself to being alone, yet another thing that set me apart from the others.

As I stride down the tower steps, I notice through a

small window a crescent moon climbing the inky expanse of sky. I pause a moment to look at it, then take a deep breath and let it out. I need to focus on my mission. No distractions.

I continue onward, and I'm halfway down the tower when I hear footsteps behind me.

Kieran steps into view and the heat of his dragon washes into me, burning brighter than the torches set along the wall. "There *is* something else," he says, his voice a deep rumble as his beast surges beneath the surface.

My heart goes from thrumming to stillness as I watch the golden glow of his eyes. "Yes?"

"Don't be a martyr, Zara." Kieran steps up so close to me that his hip brushes against mine. "I want you to come back to me." He reaches out a hand and cups my cheek in his palm. "Do you understand?"

I feel a flare of magic in my stomach, a slow spin of heat and effervescence. With trembling fingers, I reach out and place my hand over Kieran's heart. "I understand."

Kieran's hand slides down my arm and he winds his fingers through mine. His other arm snakes around my waist and he lifts and spins me into the wall. The hard length of his body presses against me as his lips hover over mine. When I wind my fist into his tunic and pull him closer, he growls and closes the last bit of distance between us.

He tastes like fire, and I can feel the heat of his dragon merge with my darker magic. With his arms holding me tightly and his chest and hips crushing against me as he claims my mouth, I feel like I am being completely and utterly consumed. My heart beats against his and power swirls within me, wrapping around us.

Just when I feel like I might burn up from the intensity of it, Kieran pulls back. He kisses me one more time, soft and sweet. "I wish we had more time," he says, his voice thick and velvety. "I've dreamed of this moment, Zara."

"So have I," I murmur. "I never knew…"

I pause, trying to find the right words, when a boom in the distance stops me. A boom followed almost instantly by screams and yells. Kieran and I spin toward the sound at the same time.

"The Daemonium," he says, a growl in his voice. "You need to go. Remember what I said. No martyrs."

"No martyrs," I repeat.

Our eyes meet one last time, and then, pulling shadows around me, I blur down the stairs. Once in the courtyard, I take a set of steps to the rooftop of the adjacent building. I head south away from the river, away from the sounds of battle. I've already decided what I'm going to use to gain an audience with the Lord of Night, but first I need information.

I pause once on the edge of Animus territory, murmuring a quick prayer to the dark goddess for my faction. I'm not even sure if I believe in her, but tonight, when my house goes to war without me, it can't hurt. After the words leave my lips, I tear my eyes from my home and continue into the outskirts of the city.

I stick to the rooftops as I travel. Even though it's not

late, there aren't many people out and about. They can hear the battle same as I can, and they're tucked inside their houses, safe and sound. At least, as safe as one can be in Night. A graveyard stretches below, and I skirt around it. I pass more churches, more homes, some small and quaint, others large and sprawling. Huge oak trees spring up here and there in odd places, growing in such a way that it's obvious they weren't meant to be there. So many parts of the city are deserted or destroyed due to the war. Nature has slowly reclaimed this place, and in less populated areas, where no one fought her back, she's crept in. Buildings covered entirely in ivy. Wildflowers growing in alleyways high as your hip. It seems right, somehow. A return to what was.

After a couple hours traveling south, and then a bit west, I draw close to the perimeter of the city. From my vantage point atop an old battlement, I can see the Waste beyond, about a quarter mile away. It starts as gray, cracked earth, but not far past that the fog sets in. Even from this distance, I can hear, very faintly, the strange hum of it. I don't know what causes the hum. No one does. But it's there, ever-present, as are the flickering pockets of wild magic, or sometimes a flash in the depths like lightning.

I have no desire to traverse the Waste, however. My destination lies right at the border, so close that almost no one dares go there. It makes normal people uncomfortable to venture along the edge. Some even say there are monsters living in the fog, monsters that will come snatch you off into the Waste to devour your bones. But the only monsters I've seen live right here in this city.

I hop down to street level in front of a large shamble of a building next to a field. It looks like it used to be a stable of sorts, constructed of stone and wood with a shallow tiled roof and a weathervane at the top. A sign hangs by rusty chains over the front door, lit from behind by two lanterns burning with purple orbs of magic. The sign says *Siduri's Tavern*.

Over these last ten years, I've served the Animus as a spy. Not Kieran's only spy, but generally regarded as the best. They all assume I'm a good spy because of my shadow magic, and that's certainly a huge part of it. But there's another weapon at my disposal, one I never told anyone about, not even Lyri.

The rebels Jaylen and I lived with after our parents died used to come to this tavern, a hangout for the Faction-less. Those who answer to no one but themselves. A cauldron of thieves, cutthroats, and gamblers. My roots and my upbringing. I suppose it's cheating a bit, getting my intel at a place like this when I don't have time to sneak around in the darkness. But all good spies have their secrets.

And sometimes, it just comes down to who you know.

CHAPTER
SIX
ZARA

When I slide into a seat at the smooth wooden bar, the woman behind it glances up from where she's pouring golden liquid into a shot glass. "Where the hell have you been all these months?"

The tavern is crowded, but most of the customers are spread out at tables throughout the room, with only a couple at the bar itself. It's as rustic inside as it is outside: large old barrels standing upright with plywood for tables, lanterns hanging on old chains from the ceiling. Smoke in a variety of colors rises from pipes and rolled cigarettes, and here and there sparkling dust from something a bit more exotic.

A smile flickers at the corners of my mouth. "Just the usual, Sidi."

She passes the shot to another customer, an Angelus with lavender wings. "I hope you don't think you're going to show up here after all this time and shake down my people for information." I roll my eyes, and Sidi grins. "At least, not after having a drink with me."

"Just one," I say in a warning tone. "Unless you want me dead later tonight. I can't lose my edge."

"Sounds dangerous, darling." She winks and begins to pour the golden liquor into two new glasses. "How fabulous."

"We'll see."

I've known Sidi since I was a child and I trust her more than I trust most people, though I don't trust anyone entirely. I wrap my fingers around the glass she hands me, within which is a significantly bigger pour than the one she gave the angel. Apparently she *is* trying to get me killed.

Sidi clinks her glass to mine and tosses back her whole drink in one long chug. I take half of it, and when she glares, I hastily finish the other half. It burns my throat and flames through my chest. The room sparkles briefly before dimming again. Sidi's homemade liquor isn't for the faint of heart, but I know she won't talk until I appease her.

"So," she says, leaning forward on one arm and running a hand through her short silver hair with the other. "What kind of trouble did you find this time? Tell me this isn't about the allegiance ball drama…"

I stare at her meaningfully for a moment until she groans.

"Of course it is." A sigh.

"I need to know who planned the attack from the Syreni side. The name of their head Incantrix." My eyes meet hers as I slowly spin my glass on the bar. "Assuming they did not die at the ball."

"Are you going to kill them?"

I shrug.

"Never mind. I don't want to know." Another sigh. She lowers her voice so no one else can hear us. "Though I wish you weren't doing all this for one of the faction leaders. They're all the same. Not a good one in the lot."

"We've been through this…" Sidi is the only one who knows where I live and who I work for. The others in this place wouldn't be so understanding. Not that she is, either. But she hasn't tried to kill me yet.

"I know. The handsome Kieran of House Animus is your tutor and you think you need him." Sidi rolls her eyes.

I pointedly ignore her, though hearing Kieran's name makes my stomach spin. "So, what have you heard?"

"The witch you're looking for goes by Selena." Sidi always uses the old slang word for the Incantrix, even though she is one herself. "She lives on the island with the others who work for the Mer."

I nod. The island is a thin strip of land in the middle of the river on the west side of the city. I could have guessed as much, but it's good to have someone confirm it, because it's not going to be easy to get on and off the thing in one piece. It's highly defensible on any day, not to mention the Syreni and their Incantrix are no doubt on high alert after their failed assassination attempt. I wouldn't be surprised if they're under attack tonight like the Animus.

Every bit of it makes what I'm going to do a thousand times more difficult.

"Thanks," I say to Sidi.

She slaps the smooth wood between us. "Your turn. Pay up."

Sidi and I don't exchange money, only information. So, for my part I share all the intel with her that I can. Which is everything I've gathered during my spying since I saw her last, except the details of my current mission. But she knows better than to think I'll share that.

When I'm done, Sidi says, "The Animus who died last night—a friend of yours?" I go still, and the look on my face tells her everything. "Oh, love…I'm so sorry."

Her hand twitches toward mine, but she stops short of touching me. Sidi and I go way back, but we're not that sort of friend. I fight the wave of black agony that rises in my chest, shoving it down to swirl in my core along with my magic. I will need every ounce of this pain later. But for now, it must wait.

Instead she says, "There are reports of deaths all across the city, not just those at the ball. Apparently, the Lord of Night's blast of power had much wider repercussions."

I scowl. It's not the first time such a thing has happened—sometimes, inexplicably, the wild magic surges and claims lives all across Night, all at once. I've long wondered what caused it, and it doesn't come as a huge surprise, but it still unsettles me. No one should have so much power at their disposal. It makes my mission even more crucial.

Several irritated calls from across the room break through my discussion with Sidi. She straightens and hurls a rude comment in response, adding an unsavory gesture with her hand.

"I'd best get back to work," she says with a sigh. "War brews tonight, and that always makes the people thirsty."

"Thanks for your help. And the drink. As always."

"Be safe, Zara."

I slide off the bar stool and make my way back through the crowded room and out into the night once again.

It takes me an hour or so to close in on the island in the river. I hear confirmation of my suspicions from a half mile away—there's a battle going on. Screams ring through the air along with the sound of something battering into something else, sending a resounding tremor that I can feel in the stone beneath my feet, as well as a vibration in the magic of the city. Soon I have a line of sight and can see the cause of it, Daemonium blasting spells into the magical barrier the Incantrix on the island have erected. Smoke and sulfur tinge the night air.

I pause in the shadow of an oak tree just outside the melee, going through options in my head. I feel confident I can make it to the island unseen. Finding the right witch and bringing her back with me is an entirely different story. Waiting until the battle is over is the safer choice, but that would involve sitting on my heels while my faction is under attack on the other side of the city. I know either way I can't prevent the loss of life that will inevitably happen tonight, but if I sit this one out, it's going to feel like their blood is on my hands.

With a groan, I push myself off the tree. I pull my focus and move through the night, as weightless as the shadows surrounding me. Within moments I reach the ranks of Daemonium, lined up along the banks of the river throwing everything they have, weapons physical and magical alike, at the island. Bursts of colored light and balls of fire fly through the air before smashing into an invisible barrier that domes over the island. Where they hit, the sky ripples and a pale silver shimmer illuminates the spell protecting the Incantrix.

The Daemonium are too focused on the attack to notice a shiver in the shadows as I move among them, swiftly but carefully, ready to change course in an instant. Which happens several times—the Incantrix aren't just sitting on the island huddled beneath their forcefield. They're on the offensive, too, blasting their own spells into the ranks of their attackers. Twice I have to dodge a ball of magic bigger than a cauldron as it flies through the crowd. One of them rolls so close to me that I inhale several hot sparks of magic. Pain lances through my head and I stagger, nearly colliding with one of the Daemonium. I catch myself at the last moment, and then I am at the riverbank.

I jump off the stone wall onto the lower bank below, landing in a crouch. I stay down a moment, surveying the scene before me. The Daemonium are swarming like hornets around the entrance to the stone bridge across the river, the one that goes to the island and then across to

Angelus territory. There's no pushing past them. I can't slide through where bodies are packed so close together. Not without someone noticing.

My eyes travel down to the water. The Syreni aren't letting their Incantrix fight alone. Several dozen dot the surface of the river, their head or chest above water, hurling their own magic at the Daemonium. It's only a short distance across the water to the island, and the Mer are spread far enough apart that I can move between them, as long as I don't disturb the water and give myself away. I jog away from the crush of bodies at the bridge.

I call on my magic and I zip across the surface of the water, a blur of shadow skimming from one bank to the next. Within moments I reach the island and climb up onto the grassy slope there. Taking a breath to center myself, I walk slowly forward, wrapped in darkness, *listening*. I need to find the Incantrix named Selena. Which is a bit challenging with magic being blasted back and forth and people yelling and things exploding.

A half hour later I've circled the small island, getting a count of the Incantrix there and a feel for their magic. Each one I pass has a different level of power running through them. Selena must be very strong and high-ranking to have led the attack on the Lord of Night. I narrow it down to one of three women, based on the strength of the magic I feel coming off them. Then I narrow it further, to one of two women who seem to be directing the others.

When another quarter hour passes and no one calls to

either of the women in such a way that I can identify them, I decide to take matters into my own hands.

"Selena!" I scream from behind the two of them.

The blonde woman on the right, who is standing atop a short stone wall, whips her head in my direction. When she sees no one, she looks left and right, her brow wrinkling. Then she turns back to the chaos before her and yells more orders to the Incantrix hurling spells below her.

Now comes the hard part.

I stride forward, a swell of magic burning in my chest, one hand outstretched. I'll need to knock her out quickly and then conceal her in shadows, too. I've never cloaked anyone but myself, so I'm hoping it'll work the same way.

Five feet from the wall I let magic blast from my fingertips toward the Incantrix who's going to be my ticket into the inner circle of the Lord of Night.

At that same moment, I feel someone else's magic right behind me, but it's too late. Something knocks me in the back of the head and darkness claims me.

CHAPTER
SEVEN
ZARA

T he song wraps around me like a tangible thing, sweet and soft and fragile. The chords twang at my heart as if I am the instrument, sending vibrations through my chest, my stomach, my throat. An undercurrent of power pulses through it, and the impression of a vast, glowing, violet light. Emotion so strong it makes my eyes prick with tears. Sadness and longing and *loneliness...*

Something yanks me backward, away from the warm darkness and the purple glow.

Light begins to sparkle at the edges of my vision, and my head swims. I reenter my body in a rush. Hard stone beneath my knees. Arms twisted behind my back and bound. Cool night air carrying the scent of the river. Voices all around me. And magic. Magic from at least a dozen Incantrix.

Then I feel another presence approaching. Magic as

radiant as the sun. Power I'd recognize anywhere.

"We have your witch!" yells a female voice. "Call off your demons or we will kill her!"

Cold steel presses against my throat, biting into my skin. A metallic tang fills the air as my blood spills, just a few drops. My vision finally clears.

I'm on the bridge. Selena has me on my knees before a throng of Daemonium. She clearly thinks I'm working for the Lord of Night. If I weren't about to die, I'd have to laugh at the irony. Because it's not the blade that's going to kill me. It's the ruler of the city, who is now making his way slowly toward us, his soldiers parting for him to pass.

And since, of course, he has no idea who I am, someone is going to slaughter me on this bridge.

Instinct and wild magic take over, that call of Night within, and magic explodes out of me like a bomb detonating.

Selena and the other Incantrix surrounding me fly backwards. The blade slices deeper into my throat for a moment before clattering to the stones beneath me. The Daemonium standing a dozen feet away are knocked off their feet as well. I wrap shadows around me, disappearing from view, and I spin to run in the opposite direction. That way lies Angelus territory, but it's better than what faces me on the other side of the bridge.

Except when I turn, the Lord of Night is standing right in front of me. How did he move that fast?

He towers over me. Clearly, he can see through my shadows. His eyes lock onto mine from behind that same silver mask he wore at the ball. They're a deep metallic brown, like tea leaves swirled with copper. He inhales deeply as if taking in my scent, and his eyes dart to my neck. His hand stretches toward me, and I think for a moment he's going to touch the wound there, but his fingers rest on my shoulder instead. A pulse of magic moves between us, and the Lord's eyes glow purple for a moment.

"You will come with me," he says. He speaks softly, but his voice is deep and dark and ancient like the catacombs. Like earth and night combined. "If you try to escape again, you will not care for the consequences."

He doesn't wait for an indication that I understand. His fingers slide from my shoulder, and he strides past me. My heart hammers in my chest, and I have only a half moment to make my decision. Not that there's any decision to make.

I only have one option.

I spin and jog to close the two-stride distance between us, walking at the Lord of Night's shoulder as we exit the bridge. The Incantrix are still lying stunned on the stones, along with most of the Daemonium, though they were further away from the blast radius. After we pass, I hear footsteps as the Daemonium who are still standing rush forward to deal with the enemy. Whether they are imprisoning them or killing them, I do not know. I don't look back.

Once we reach the riverbank, the crowd of Daemonium warriors begins to move aside as the ones on the bridge had. Their eyes land heavily upon me as I follow their leader, no doubt wondering who I am. I force myself to take deep breaths, bringing the autumnal night air in and out of my lungs. I need to focus.

A few moments ago, I was sure my life was about to end. I'd been strangely emotionless in that moment, staring into the face of death. But now, knowing that my moment has not come, the rush of feelings is intense. I'm walking shoulder-to-shoulder with the man who killed my sister. The man I've hated for more than a decade. I'd known it would be hard to get close to him, but I'm still unprepared for the all-consuming rage and sorrow that storm through me.

I dig my fingernails into my palms to center myself. My plan has gone wildly sideways, but maybe I can salvage this. This is what I wanted, after all. To have an audience with the Lord of Night, to convince him to let me work for him. I have that chance now, even if it came about in an entirely unexpected way.

We reach the upper bank, and out of the night a huge horse comes into view. Gray, like rain or steel or the shadows on the moon. He snorts and tosses his head, his hooves clattering on the stone.

Hands wrap around my waist, and I suck in a sharp breath as the Lord of Night lifts me onto the back of the creature. He swings up into the saddle in front of me a moment later and the horse leaps forward. I have no choice but to wrap my arms around his torso to keep from flying off backwards. It seems a definite impropriety to touch the ruler of the city in this way, and I sincerely hope he doesn't decide to kill me for the offense. Otherwise, this will all be over a lot sooner than planned. Not that any of this is going to plan.

I can feel his muscles beneath his cloak and tunic, hard and solid. Heat pulsates off of him. The rumors say he is a hybrid of the Daemonium, which is one of the reasons for his immense power. It is said he drinks blood like the cold ones, but also possesses the magic of the wicked flame-bearers. It is definitely the latter I feel now. I can feel his heartbeat, too. The city rushes past us and everything seems intensely surreal. Maybe I did actually die on the bridge, and this is all some wild afterlife voyage.

But when the horse clatters into the courtyard at the Palace of Night a very few minutes later, and the deadly man in the saddle before me lifts me down like I weigh nothing at all, everything feels very real. The texture of the stone tiles beneath my boots. The stickiness of the blood pooling on my neck. The smoke from the torches encircling the area.

Several servants stand at the doorway the Lord strides to. They bow as he passes hurriedly, and I follow a stride behind. I catch their confused gazes as I move past. And then we are inside the palace, moving through a marble-floored ballroom, down several corridors, and finally into a room smaller than the rest. There are bookshelves lining one wall, and a fireplace opposite. The Lord of Night sits down in a large winged-back chair and gestures for me to sit opposite him in the other.

A man dressed in fine attire enters a moment later, carrying a crystal pitcher of ruby-red wine. He pours a glass for his employer and sets it down on the table between us.

"Leave us," the Lord says, the quiet, simple command of one used to being utterly obeyed.

The servant hurriedly exits the room, and the Lord of Night gets back up out of his chair and moves to a painted cabinet in the far corner of the room. He retrieves a crystal decanter of golden liquid and another glass, this one stemless. When he returns to the table, he pours a small amount of the liquor and sets it before me.

"I don't think you'll care for what I drink," he says in that voice of dark, velvet skies.

He sits back down and those molten brown eyes lock onto mine. It seems he's waiting for something, so I say, "Thank you." I force my tone to remain neutral, though it burns my soul to say anything of the sort to my most hated of enemies.

It hits me, the insanity of this plan. I don't know if I can do what Kieran has asked. Sitting here, the object of my revenge staring back at me, no more than six feet away. How am I going to look into those eyes without trying to claim what's owed to me?

The Lord of Night picks up his glass of wine and raises it to his lips. His gaze drifts to the wound on my neck as he takes a sip, then sets the glass back down.

"So, shadow wielder," he says. "We have much to discuss."

EIGHT

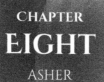

I tear my gaze from the trails of crimson running down the Incantrix's neck and raise my eyes to hers. They're a shade of purple like a certain type of orchid I once saw in a garden long ago. They match the aura of magic pulsating around her.

Never in my two hundred years have I felt anyone with magic to rival my own.

Not until tonight.

"Tell me why the Syreni thought that you were mine," I say, taking another sip of my wine. The tang of blood mixed into it calms the hunger running through me, something much needed with an open wound on a very pretty neck just an arm's span away.

She doesn't answer for a moment. Her expression is guarded, unreadable, but the magic within her swirls in an agitated manner.

"I suppose they assumed when they found an unknown

Incantrix behind their magical barrier that I was working for their attackers." Her voice is calm and level, showing no sign of fear.

I turn my head slightly to the side, intrigued. "And it was your little trick with the shadows that got you through that barrier?"

She nods.

"What were you doing there, on the island?" I tap one finger on the arm of my chair. "Seems the middle of a battle is an odd time to sneak around."

"I was looking for someone."

The raven-haired woman lifts her glass of liquor and takes a sip of it. It's the first sign that she's nervous in my presence, her first tell.

I wait for her to continue.

"The Incantrix who led the attack at the allegiance ball. My plan was to capture her and bring her back to you." She takes another sip before setting her glass down on the table.

A pulse of surprise moves through me, and surprise is not a feeling that visits me often. "How interesting. And why would you do that?"

"I'd like a job," she says without the slightest hesitation.

"I have plenty of Incantrix already."

Her eyes lock onto mine. "And none of them are like me."

A flare of heat spikes through my core, my inner demon stirring. This witch is bold. But she's not wrong.

On the bridge, I'd recognized the scent and feel of her magic right away, even before she knocked out all those Incantrix, and a good deal of my own warriors.

"You were at the allegiance ball," I say. I take another sip of my drink, forcing my hunger back. It's always there, but this walker of shadows is making it worse.

She stiffens and her eyes flare for the barest of moments.

"How do I know you weren't part of the attempt to assassinate me?"

"I just told you, I was trying to bring you the Incantrix responsible for that." Her posture and her voice have regained their stillness. "Why would I do that if I were part of the plan?"

"Then why were you there that night?"

"Reconnaissance," she says. "I was trying to figure out a way to approach you. And after the attack, I had it."

I lean back in my chair and watch her for a moment. The firelight plays over her tawny skin, making it even richer in color.

"And why would a Factionless Incantrix want to work for the ruler of the city?" Another sip of wine. "It seems antithetical to the beliefs of your kind."

She's silent for a long moment, and when she speaks, her voice has dropped an octave or two. It's both lyrical and rough, honey and thistles mixed. "Maybe I'm tired of not belonging to something that matters."

I can't tell if she's lying, and that makes me trust her even less than I did originally. Which wasn't much to begin with. But with power like hers, I can't let her walk out of here.

The smart thing to do, of course, is kill her.

Curiosity, however, is a powerful thing. I'm far too intrigued by the strength within her, magic to possibly rival even my own. I need to know more about her. I need to keep her close.

She could even be the answer I've been searching for.

No. I slam the door on that thought before it can take root. That is a wildly dangerous idea, and I can't afford such things living in my head.

"You'll have to prove yourself to me," I say, staring into those violet eyes. "Your mission tonight didn't exactly go as planned. You could even say that I saved your life."

Her jaw flexes and her eyes simmer for a moment, but she keeps her mouth shut.

"You are under my employ," I say. "On a trial basis. After that, we will reevaluate."

She nods stiffly. "Thank you."

I rise from my chair. "It's late, and you expended a great deal of magic earlier. Follow me."

I stride from the library and lead her through the familiar maze of halls. Polished floors and ornately painted walls that have faded over time. Gold filigree peeling from the crown moldings overhead. A gilded prison I can never truly escape.

My hand slides to my chest and through my tunic, I touch the black jewel hanging there, right above my heart. I'm walking ahead of my new Incantrix, so she can't see.

Magic sparks at my fingers when I touch the cool stone, and I feel the pulse of wild magic throughout Night. The hunger returns, and this time it's not just the woman at my back.

I go up a flight of stone steps to the second floor of the palace, then through a set of ornate double doors into a suite of rooms beyond. There's a large sitting room with a huge fireplace and two hallways, one on each side. I lead the Incantrix to the left. I open the first door on the right, and gesture for her to go inside.

She turns after she enters it, a question on her face.

A flicker of magic from my fingers and two lanterns light, one on each side of the room. A large four-post bed sits in the center of the far wall. "These will be your quarters."

I pivot and point back the way we came. "My quarters are on the other side of that sitting room. I need you close by, being as how you can disappear in shadows anytime you want. I imagine you're quite used to coming and going as you please."

Her eyes widen, but she says nothing.

"I can sense your magic. There's a lot of it, and it has quite a unique signature." My lips quirk up into a small smile. "So, I will know if you leave this suite without my permission."

She nods once, a sharp jerk of her chin.

I point toward a smaller door in the back corner. "There's a bath in there. Get yourself cleaned up." My eyes linger on her neck once more. "I'll send someone up with bandages and clean clothes. I'll send someone up to perform rites with as well. You depleted a lot on the bridge."

She shakes her head. "That's not necessary. The last part, that is."

We lock gazes for a moment, and I decide to let it go. At least for now. "Very well."

I turn to leave, but at the doorway, I pause. My eyes meet hers again. "What's your name, Incantrix?"

"Zara."

Names have power, as they say, and hers shivers over me with a pulse of magic. I'm not sure if I've brought an enemy or an incredibly strong asset into my home.

She's dangerous either way.

"Goodnight, Zara."

I close the door behind me on my way out.

The door closes behind the Lord of Night and I let out the breath I've been holding for an eternity.

I'm inside the Palace of Night.

Within the personal suite of the ruler of this city.

I couldn't have chosen a better place to enact my plan for revenge. After all these years, it's finally happening. As they say, be careful what you wish for. Because I'm also just paces away from the most dangerous man alive. Someone who could kill me with the snap of his fingers. Summon my life force out of me with a single glance.

He also clearly wants my blood. The rumors weren't wrong about him, he is a demon of both kinds, blood drinker and fire summoner. Every time his eyes went to my neck, I had to force myself not to panic. His predator's gaze made my heart race, made it hard not to run from the room. It was only my years living with the Animus, in a literal den of predators, that had given me the strength to withstand my impulse. And with it came the strangest sensation...

I've never been *craved* before.

I shake my head as I pace back and forth across the marble floor. Nothing about my encounter with my enemy transpired as I'd imagined it. I'd expected him to be outwardly cruel, for his magic to feel dark and tainted. But instead, he is quiet. Reserved. Curious almost. And his magic feels as mine does...within it, I can feel the pulsing heart of Night that lies beneath the city.

Someone knocks on my door and I nearly jump out of my skin.

I stride over and open it. A woman stands there, her blonde hair pulled back into a bun. She's maybe ten years older than I am and she wears a simple black dress, not the garb of a warrior. A stack of towels and bandages sits atop her outstretched arms. There is no magical aura about her, she is one of the unmagicked. I feel a surge of pity.

"Oh, thank you," I say, and try to take them from her.

She ignores my attempt at help and veers around me, heading for the bathroom in the far corner of the room. I follow behind, not sure what to do. I watch as she sets the towels on a shelf near a large clawfoot tub, and the bandages next to the sink. She turns to glance at me, her eyes traveling up and down, then after her brief appraisal she strides to the bath and turns on both faucets.

When I continue to stand in the doorway, she points

and says, "Undress. I can't bathe you with your clothes on."

"That's not necessary." I cross my arms over my chest. "I can bathe myself. But thanks."

Are there really people in the world who can't bathe themselves? I've never experienced such treatment before.

She shoots me a dubious look, but strides past me without arguing the point. "I'll be back with clean clothes."

I sit gingerly on one of the fancy chairs in my room while the tub fills, and a few minutes later the servant returns with a stack of clothes. Another woman is with her this time, carrying a tray of bread and cheese, along with a pitcher of water. The second woman eyes me warily, almost as if she's afraid. When I thank them, she flashes me a wide-eyed look and scurries from the room.

After they're gone, I strip off my boots and leather jacket and tunic, and I get into the tub. The water is deliciously hot, something we don't have in our cathedral-turned-barracks in the Animus compound. I scrub myself with soap, washing my long hair as well.

When I'm done, I put a bandage on my neck wound and dig through the pile of clean clothes. The only sleep-wear they've brought is made from a material far more silky and sheer than anything I've ever worn. It feels strange and slippery against my skin, like snake scales. I eat a bit of the food, then climb into the enormous bed. With a wave of my hand, I dim both lanterns. I feel much more comfortable in the dark.

67

Moonlight cascades through the window on the other side of the room. It's not right that I'm lying here, clean and safe in a huge bed, when my own house is under attack. How many have died tonight? And what of Kieran? He could have fallen in battle and I wouldn't even know it. I should be used to it by now—after all, we are at war every day, even if some days we hide behind a fragile truce. But it never gets easier, and here, far from home, the not knowing might drive me mad. Kieran holds the very last piece of my heart, and if that piece crumbles, what will I become?

No, there will be no sleep tonight, not now, with a battle raging on the other side of the city. Not here, with the Lord of Night on the other side of this suite.

But I should at least rest and recoup some of my energy. He was right about one thing—I did expend a lot of power on the bridge earlier. Though, I could have made my escape if he hadn't blocked me. I owe him *nothing*.

As soon as my thoughts turn to him, I realize I can sense him, as he mentioned sensing me. He has too much power pouring off him not to notice, even from this distance. I'm used to feeling the flow of magic throughout Night, but most of it lingers beneath the streets, in the earth beneath me. Being this close to him, I can almost see it through the walls, like I'm sleeping next to a huge dragon instead of a man. A giant glowing beast who ate the moon out of the sky.

Is he lying in his bed, sensing my magic, too?

A shiver whispers across my skin, and I pull the soft

bedsheets closer to my chin. I realize something as I lay there in the dark, in the palace of my mortal enemy.

Never once, from the bridge to the horseback ride to the conversation in the library, did the Lord of Night take off his silver mask.

CHAPTER
TEN
ZARA

When the sun rises, I can feel it.

I get out of bed, feeling rested enough, though I did not allow myself to fully drift to sleep at any point in the night. It was a skill I'd learned when my sister and I were in the prison camp. To sleep soundly was to be completely vulnerable to your enemies. You might as well offer them your throat like a subservient dog.

I'm pleasantly surprised to see that the clothes the servants brought me fit fairly well, and are close to what I'm used to, unlike what I wore to bed. There are dark leather breeches and a form-fitting tunic. I don't care for the deep wine color, as opposed to my usual black, but it's clean. I pull on my boots and jacket over the top.

There's a knock on the door not long after, a man bringing food. More bread and cheese, and a bit of sliced meat this time. I eat quickly as I debate what happens next. Do I just sit here until the Lord of Night summons me to perform whatever test of skills he has in mind? It feels far too much like I'm some sort of prisoner. Yet, the idea of leaving the room and wandering around in his suite seems equally unnerving.

I finish my breakfast and have begun to pace the room while debating the merits and drawbacks of both options when there's another knock at the door. When I open it, I come face to face with a Daemonium.

She has long, dark hair like mine, though perhaps more a shade of auburn than obsidian. Eyes the deep red of rubies and fresh blood. Skin pale as stars. I can tell from the feel of her magic, as well as her eyes, that she's one of the fire types, not one of the cold ones who drink blood. Though, she has no visible horns or wings like some of the fire summoners.

"Zara," she says, scanning me pointedly up and down with those red eyes. "I'm Tryn. I've been assigned as your guardian during your… training period."

I can't quite read the tone in which she says the last two words. It seems an odd mix of intrigue and disdain. "Nice to meet you," I say, just to be polite.

Based on her thin smile, I'm quite sure the feeling is not mutual. "Follow me. We'll start with a tour of the palace and grounds." She jerks her head toward the hall and marches off without waiting to see if I follow.

As we pass through the sitting room between our

suites, I cast my gaze around, wondering if the Lord of Night is nearby.

"He's not here," Tryn says.

A shiver runs over me. Before I can wonder how I hadn't noticed the gigantic power source that is the Lord of Night had left at some point, we're out of the suite and striding down a long hallway. We head to the first floor of the palace, and to the west. After traveling through the beehive of intersecting halls on the first floor, Tryn turns into a huge room filled with steam and ovens and giant cauldrons boiling over wrought-iron stoves.

"The kitchen," she says with a bored wave of her hand. "You'll have food brought to you regularly, but just in case you get hungry another time."

We pass through the kitchen and out a door on the other side, then down another long hallway. As we start passing doorways that appear to lead to bedrooms, Tryn says, "These are the living quarters of the Daemonium. The Incantrix stay in the wing on the other side of the palace." She gestures in that direction. "You *should* be staying there."

Soon we turn into an adjacent wing of the palace, a short one that connects the two long parallel wings framing the courtyard. Based on what Tryn said, the Daemonium all stay in the northern wing, and the Incantrix in the southern wing opposite. Through an open window, my eyes drift down to the courtyard where the Lord sat two nights before at the ball. Images fill my head: Lyri dragging me to safety. The attack. Her body lying on the stone, her essence ripped out of it. A shiver runs over me, and I can feel Tryn's eyes on mine.

Clenching my fingers into a fist, nails cutting into my palms, I bring myself back.

"Where do you practice?" I ask her.

"You read my mind," she says with a smirk, exiting a door to our right.

We enter a second courtyard, this one even larger than the one where the ball was held. Dozens of Daemonium and Incantrix dot the space, sparring either with fists or weapons or magic. Tryn leads me right into the middle of it, through the clusters of warriors. As we move, eyes follow me and some of the warriors stop what they're doing to stare. The looks they shoot me are decidedly unfriendly.

Tryn finally stops in the middle of the courtyard before a tall woman with long red hair braided down her back. One of her eyes is bright red, the other a shocking shade of purple.

"This is our drill master, Aya Olora," Tryn says. She offers the woman a small bow.

The woman nods her head in greeting, then her eyes land on mine. "The warriors call me Master Olora, and you will do the same."

She circles me, and I feel a flare of heat and magic. The sensation of her power confirms what I suspected from her mismatched eyes: she is both Daemonium and

Incantrix. Her predator vibes are nearly as strong as the Lord of Night, but I control my instincts and force myself to stand still as she looks me up and down like I'm some sort of livestock.

"Our Lord wants you tested," Master Olora says. "So, test you we shall."

A prickle moves over my scalp as Olora calls out across the courtyard. "Who wants to challenge this initiate?"

The crowd has drawn in around us, and I feel the press of nearly a hundred magical auras. I'm surrounded by my enemies, a stranger and an outcast in a sea of malevolence. Whatever the Lord of Night told his warriors about why he brought me here and what he plans to do, they are clearly not enthused. Is it because I'm an outsider? Or is it because he's never done such a thing before, bringing someone here and housing them in his personal quarters? Tryn implied as much.

Several hands shoot up across the crowd, and Master Olora waves them forward. They step into the small circle that's formed around me. Tryn melts back into the crowd, an amused look on her face. I decide then that I hate her, not that I care much for any of them.

There are five volunteers, three Daemonium and two Incantrix. One of the Daemonium has solid black eyes and golden horns protruding from its forehead, and another stands about seven feet tall, with leathery brown wings like a bat. Not that the three without such features are any less dangerous. Their eyes burn into me, and magic ripples around the circle.

I expect Master Olora to pick one of them to pair up with me first, but she simply steps back and gestures to all six of us.

"Begin."

CHAPTER
ELEVEN

ASHER

When I return from meeting with my generals to get an update on the battles from the night before, I instantly feel the swell of power from the practice yard. A magic that can only be one thing.

I stride along the second-floor corridors until I come to a gallery with several open arches overlooking the training space. Below me, in the center, I see five of the warriors sparring with Zara. Sparring being too mild a term for the all-out battle taking place between them. Five against one is hardly a fair fight.

My fingers crush the stone wall beneath me as I fight the urge to intervene. I feel a strange sense of protective-ness over my new Incantrix, which is an odd emotion given she could quite possibly best me in a fight. And given that I don't trust her as far as I can throw her. But I'd told Aya Olora to test her, and I can't disrupt that process now. I've caused enough of a stir by bringing Zara back to the palace in the first place, let alone keeping her in my personal quarters. The rumors have been flying faster than comets.

I watch Zara, studying the movement of her body and magic both. She's a seasoned warrior, well-trained. I'd assumed she was Factionless since I'd found her solo in enemy territory, but someone has clearly tutored her. Maybe she'd grown up in one of the houses after all, had deserted at some point. Or, of course, maybe she's still working for one of them.

None of it matters. She's here now, and I cannot afford to let her go.

As she moves, whether offensively or defensively, she blends magicality and physicality perfectly. She uses her magic to make her move faster, strike harder, jump higher. She calls on shadow to morph in and out of sight, which is impressive considering it's broad daylight. Once or twice, she even loses physicality entirely, dodging a blow because it simply passes right through her.

What's more, I can tell she's holding back.

My initial desire to protect her was needless, because she can obviously take out all five of these warriors if she wants to. But she isn't for some reason. Is she afraid she's going to harm them? Or is her only next-level move another stunt like the one she pulled on the bridge last night, out of control and undisciplined?

Five minutes pass, then ten. She could have taken them in two. Why is she letting it drag on? Even the crowd around her is getting restless, and Aya looks more displeased than usual, her lips pursed in an angry scowl. She sees what I see, and I can tell she isn't happy that this new recruit outshines so many of her best fighters.

In my agitation, I walk further out along the gallery, strolling past the open arches as I stare down at the scene below. Watching Zara, feeling that magic flaring inside her just waiting to be unleashed, causes a flare of hunger inside me. As if sensing it, sensing *me*, her head whips up to where I'm standing. And in that moment of distraction, one of the Daemonium charges her and knocks her back against the stone tiles. Her head hits the ground hard and lolls to the side.

The rage is immediate and all-consuming. If that horned beast has killed Zara, I will kill *all* of them.

I wrap magic around me and vanish myself down to the courtyard below. Aya is already crouched by Zara, trying to revive her, and when I stalk toward them, her eyes flick up to me uneasily. The crowd moves away from me, everyone stepping back to give my roiling magical aura some space.

"My Lord," Aya says softly as I kneel opposite her over Zara's unconscious body.

She doesn't apologize, and I don't chastise her. We've known each other a very long time, and she knows how livid I am.

I lift Zara's head from the stone. There's no blood at the back of her head, though it radiates heat from the impact. She's breathing still, though her heartbeat is unsteady. I summon magic to the fingertips of my free hand and reach forward to touch her forehead.

I'm an inch from her face when her eyes open and her magic flares out. Her arm flies up to strike me in her panic before she sees who it is.

"I suppose this means you're going to live," I growl, blocking her blow.

I turn my gaze to the Daemonium who tackled her to the ground, my eyes telling him that he's also escaped death this day. His face storms over and he sinks back into the crowd.

I help Zara to her feet. She wobbles for a moment before steadying herself. My eyes move to Aya's. "I'll take it from here."

She clenches her jaw but nods and bows her head.

Then my eyes move to Zara's. "Follow me. Your training for the day is far from over."

TWELVE

ZARA

My head swims as I follow the Lord of Night across the courtyard. I fought off five of his warriors for over a quarter hour, and he's disappointed?

The first thing I'd seen when I'd come to was his face hovering right over mine, and he'd looked angry. As if he wanted to knock me out a second time. It was his fault I'd gotten distracted in the first place. His magic… it's not just that it's incredibly strong and burns brighter than the sun, but it… *connects* with mine.

I hadn't grasped the fullness of it the night before, but today, when I'd felt his magic flare, it tugged at my own power. A nearly physical sensation, like the strings of a harp being plucked. I've never experienced something like that with another. Why does his magic feel like my own, like the life that runs within Night?

My thoughts are interrupted when the Lord opens a

door leading into a small walled courtyard off the larger one. His expression is unreadable as he gestures for me to step inside. It seems his anger has passed, now he just seems cold and withdrawn. Looking around, I see we're in a garden, or rather, what once was a garden. I'm not sure that term can be used for the unkempt cascade of vines and flowers surrounding me, though to me, its wildness only makes it more beautiful.

The Lord strides ahead of me again, moving to an arched doorway on the far side that's nearly hidden in gray-green vines. As I walk I cast my gaze around, wide-eyed in wonder. I feel the Lord's eyes land on me when he reaches the archway, and I blush when I realize he caught me staring. I walk more quickly, and there's a flicker in those molten eyes before he turns and leads me through the door.

For a moment all I see is darkness.

Then the Lord raises his hand and lanterns ignite along the path before us. A path which leads down beneath the earth. The smell of dirt and bones hits my nose, and I realize we're in the catacombs of the Palace of Night. I walk behind the Lord as we descend deeper and deeper. Goosebumps rise along my arms as it occurs to me that I'm walking into a literal crypt with the most dangerous creature alive. Maybe what happened in the courtyard means I've failed his job interview. He could be taking me down here to kill me, and no one would ever know.

With Lyri gone, there is no one to mourn me. Except for Kieran, and I'm still not sure exactly how he feels about us after the other night. Does he still view me as just his pupil? Or did our kiss change anything?

I shiver as we step into a huge room at the bottom of the seemingly endless staircase. More lanterns flare to life around the perimeter of the room. I can see crypts set into the walls on each side of the room, rectangles of stone with ornate metal handles. Beneath each of them lie vases, some silver, some onyx, some set with bright jewels. I imagine they once held flowers, but now they are empty and covered in dust and time.

Being here among the resting place of the dead makes me realize that I don't know exactly how old the Lord of Night is. While the races of the four great houses are long-lived, spanning hundreds of years, none of us are immortal. The war has cut short countless lives over the centuries. I just know that he's ruled for as long as anyone can remember, just as this war has gone on for as long as anyone can remember. They don't exactly give us warriors history lessons. Our history is in rumors and fables passed around taverns and campfires.

On the far side of the room is a structure that looks like a small marble temple with broad white steps up the front. No doubt the crypt for someone important, which again makes me wonder about the past. I can't see within, it's just blackness beyond the open door. And further, behind the temple, something glows at the back of the catacombs, pale like moonlight. The source of the light is blocked by the temple since it spans almost the entire width of the underground space.

What lies there?

And more importantly, why has the Lord of Night brought me here?

As if reading my thoughts, he turns abruptly to face me. I almost run into him, stopping a couple of inches from his chest. Our eyes meet, and I feel that same zing of connection via our magic.

"You were holding back up there in the courtyard. Why?" He sounds angry again.

"What makes you think I was holding back?" I narrow my eyes. "I was fighting off five of your warriors. That's not exactly the best odds."

"You could have taken them in less than a minute, yet you let it carry on for fifteen. Before nearly getting yourself killed." He crosses his huge arms over his chest, staring at me from behind his silver mask.

I want to take a step back from the intensity of his gaze, but I won't give him the satisfaction. I grind my teeth together and dig my fingernails into my palms to control my temper. "Well, maybe I didn't want to kill a bunch of your warriors on my first day. Seems that would start things off on the wrong foot."

"Are you telling me you can't disable an opponent without killing them?"

"My magic is…stronger than most."

His gaze flickers. "So, you admit you *were* holding back."

"I'm always holding back!" I snap, and my magic flares.

84

Instead of the anger I expect at my outburst, a small smile tugs at his lips. He gestures to the room around us. "That's why we're here. Just you and me. No one watching. No one listening. And I promise you, you don't have to hold back with me."

I stare at him. "You want me to spar with you?"

The Lord of Night shakes his head. "I do not want to spar. I want you to attack me with everything you have."

"I could kill you."

"Kill *me*?"

I realize the deadly error of my words. A rumble moves over him, and he takes another step forward, so this time I have no choice but to back up.

"You are possibly the most arrogant person I've ever met," he growls. "Attack me. If you can disable me, then you have a job. That is my requirement."

My thoughts swirl. I will *never* get another opportunity like this. Alone with my enemy, far beneath the earth. It's as if the dark goddess has handed me my sweet revenge on a silver platter. He's even pretty much given me permission to kill him.

If I can.

But if I kill him now, I'm disobeying Kieran's orders. Betraying my commander and my house. Where does my loyalty lie? My long-sought vengeance or the man who taught me everything?

I don't have time to contemplate it further, because the Lord of Night, having clearly grown tired of waiting for me to attack, does so himself.

It's just a small lash of power, but it blasts me backwards several feet as it rockets into my torso. Pain radiates up my spine. I grit my teeth and manage to stay on my feet, sliding on the smooth stone floor, calling magic to steady me. As soon as I'm stable, I raise my hands and summon my own pulse of power. I feel it connect from the earth beneath me, that swell of magic that is Night, my constant companion. I launch it directly at the Lord of Night.

He deflects it with a mere flick of his fingers. "Come now, Zara. Why would I let you into my service if this is how you're going to fight?"

Another ball of magic flies toward me, but I block it this time and it bounces into the wall, taking out a lantern. I counterattack immediately, calling more power this time, summoning from the darkness around me, shadow and bone and earth mixed.

It flies toward the Lord, but he cast it sideways again. He smiles, taunting me. "I've saved you twice now. Last night, and now today in the courtyard. You're running up quite a tab."

Rage flares through me, and my magic pulses outward like it had on the bridge. The Lord flips onto his back on the stone floor and I stalk forward, hand outstretched, keeping him pinned to the floor. When I reach him, I stand over him, one boot on each side of his chest. If I just keep *pushing*, this will all be over. My magic flares, glowing violet around me, and my arm shakes as indecision wars within me…

I feel his fingers at my ankle a moment too late, and then I'm on my back on the stone for a second time today. The Lord of Night flips himself on top of me, straddling my hips as his magic sizzles against mine, sparks shooting off to either side of us from the friction of our power colliding. The heavy weight of his body contrasts with the electric heat of his magic. Beneath the earth, I feel the immense power that is Night rumble...

Calling on that wild source essence, I let it move through me without the careful control I've always maintained in the past. I open the door to myself wider than I ever have before. Power rushes into me, and I roll and flip the Lord of Night onto his back again. Now I'm straddling him, my hands on his hands, pinning them down. I realize in the shift that his mask has fallen off, it lies shimmering a few feet away.

Surprise shivers through me. I'd expected him to have some kind of scar or burn or deformity hiding beneath the mask. But I can't see anything other than small scars here and there. His dark hair falls around him, loose now without the mask, not quite to his shoulders. His jaw is covered in stubble, strong and square. I realize I'm staring because I didn't expect him to be beautiful. Someone so evil shouldn't look like this.

But that's the thing about demons, isn't it?

Hatred burns through my veins. *Now*. I end this now...

The wild magic is still coursing through me, rushing like heat and flame through my bones, my *soul*. The Lord of Night's eyes flare wide as he realizes what's happening.

I realize I can't shut the door to this magic now that I've opened it. That's why before I only ever cracked it the slightest bit. Now it's racing through me, and I realize with a strange detachment that I'm going to get my wish.

The Lord of Night will perish tonight.

But I'm going to burn with him.

CHAPTER
THIRTEEN

ASHER

I stare at Zara in wonder. I'd known she was powerful, one of a kind. But I hadn't realized she was *this* powerful.

She can speak to Night as I can, act as its conduit. If I'd known, I wouldn't have taunted her so. Though I realize as soon as the thought passes through my head that it's a lie. I've been searching for someone like Zara for two hundred years. Had I known, it wouldn't have stopped me from testing her.

Even though it's a flirtation with death.

Panic rolls through her eyes as she stares at me, realizing she can't stop the wild magic that is Night. I'd told her to give me everything she had, and she'd obeyed. I'm to blame for what happens next.

Her hands are crushing mine to the floor, her strength enhanced with the immense force rushing through her. Carefully, using my own power, I intertwine my fingers with hers. Our palms touch, heat rushing between them. Zara's eyes widen.

"Zara," I say softly. "Let me take some of it. The magic."

"What do you mean?" she gasps, flinching as the waves of power moving through her intensify.

"I won't hurt you. I'm just going to take some of it." I keep my voice steady, calm. If she feels threatened right now, we're both dead.

"You want to drink from me?"

Another pulse of power, and this time we both wince. Pain lances through my body like hot blades.

"If I don't take some of it, we're both going to die."

"But if you take my soul, like you did to—" She cuts off, and a whimper rises from her lips as the magic burns her. Her eyes are glowing like stars now, violet and deadly.

"Not your soul. Just some of the extra magic."

Night flares beneath us, and Zara cries out and collapses on top of me, her arms giving out. We roll to our sides and her eyes meet mine, agony reflected there. Even her skin is glowing now, as if she's about to burst from the inside out. She gives me a small, weak nod.

I wrap my arms around her and open myself, drinking in her magic. For a moment the pain intensifies as I take in the deluge of magic. But then it starts to taper off, enough so that Zara can shut the door to what she'd awakened. The moment I feel her close herself off to it, I release my hold on her and we fall away from each other, panting on the floor.

It feels like I've consumed an entire storm system, clouds, thunder, lightning and all.

When I've had a moment to catch my breath, I roll back over onto my side to face her. "Are you okay?"

She nods weakly, her eyes closed, chest rising and falling with effort, a fine tremor moving through her limbs. We lie like that for several minutes, then I climb to my feet. I try to offer her a hand, but she ignores it.

When she stands, she turns to face me, her eyes wary. "So, did I pass your test?"

"Indeed, you did." I stare down at her. "Though now that's three times I've saved your life."

She frowns, and anger flashes through those purple eyes. Her tone drips with derision. "If it makes My Lord happy to keep tallies of such things, I suppose now that I'm in your employ I'll have to start a tally of my own. And the courtyard doesn't count. I wasn't going to die."

I dip my head in concession. "Two and a half, then."

I take a step toward her, and she shoots me that suspicious look again. "We're going to be spending a lot of time together. I'd prefer you drop the formalities and call me by my name. Asher."

Surprise flashes over her face but she nods. I bend down to retrieve my silver mask, and when I straighten, I put it back in place over my eyes. Zara's own eyes flicker with a range of emotions as she watches me, too fast to read.

I lead the way back up the staircase, thoughts askew. I'd known I needed to keep Zara close the moment I met her. But now, after what happened here in the catacombs? She's the only other true conduit of Night, more dangerous than the commanders of all the warring factions combined. She'll either be my salvation, or my annihilation.

Only one thing I know for sure.

She is *mine* now, and she changes everything.

FOURTEEN

"Rest. I will summon you later," Asher says as he closes the door of my room behind him.

Asher. I'm on first name basis with the man I hate more than anything in this world.

A maelstrom of emotions spins me as I stalk across the room, ripping off my jacket and hurling it to the floor. I can feel a scream building in my core, and knowing I can't release it just makes it burn inside me even hotter. Magic glows along my skin, pulsating like a firefly as I pace back and forth.

I can still feel Asher's fingers intertwined with mine, the rush of heat where our palms touched.

I *hate* him. I hate him even more now, which I never dreamed possible. I'd had him right where I wanted him, held his life in my hands, and yet I couldn't take it. Weakness had claimed me. I'd realized down in the catacombs that as much as I want him dead, which I want more than anything else, I don't want to go with him.

Coward.

I'd stared into the face of death and backed away from that yawning brink. And now, I have to live with the horrible truth.

I can't kill the Lord of Night without sacrificing my own life.

I'd had to open myself to the wild magic more than I ever have before, and I'd lost control. It had consumed me, and it'd been excruciating. Betrayal simmers in my stomach. Magic has been the only constant in my life, and now I realize I've been a fool to ever think I could wield it without consequences. But most disturbing is knowing I'm not the only one Night speaks through, after all. I share that connection with *him*.

Exhaustion, both physical and emotional, drags me toward the bed. I collapse onto it, fully clothed, and within moments sleep claims me.

When I hear a knock on the door I jolt awake, hand going to the dagger at my thigh. I see darkness through the window, which means I've been asleep for hours. I can't believe I let down my guard like that. A shiver of unease runs through me.

I cross the room and open the door to see an unknown Incantrix standing there.

"Hi, Zara. I'm Elyse. The Lord sent me to check on you." She smiles, and it seems genuine enough. The first person here who hasn't looked frightened, suspicious, or outright hateful.

"Sure, come in."

I step back and gesture for her to enter. As I walk over to one of the wingback chairs near the fireplace, I see Elyse cast her eyes down at the floor where I'd thrown my jacket. Blushing, I pick it up and throw it on the bed before taking a seat. It feels strange and awkward taking visitors in my room, but I remind myself that my true mission here is to gain information about the enemy. Which requires me actually talking to people.

Elyse smiles again as she folds herself into the chair opposite me. She's a petite little thing, with hair cut short around her head. It's an odd shade of pale silver, though she looks no older than I am, and her eyes are a deep purple. She reminds me of a pixie from the old fairytales.

"Are you getting settled in here at the palace?" Elyse asks.

"Um..." Settled is opposite how I would describe things.

She must read the expression on my face because she frowns. "The other warriors can be a bit much at times. The Lord has never brought in an outsider in this manner." Her eyes widen a moment later. "Not that I'm excusing the way they've treated you."

Her expression is so remorseful that I feel a pang of pity. She must have seen the sparring in the courtyard earlier. "It's okay. I get it."

Elyse's breath rushes out in a relieved sigh. "Oh, good. Sometimes I have a knack for saying precisely the wrong thing."

I smile. "I can understand that." Which is why I say as little as possible...

"So, I guess I'm your new sponsor, so to speak," Elyse says. "If you have questions about anything, need anything. The Lord was particularly concerned that you find someone to perform your rites with, so you can recharge your energy..."

"I'm fine," I say, forcing a smile.

I'm hardly going to get naked and vulnerable in this pit of vipers. Plus, it seems a sure way to make more enemies here if my power consumes the person I'm bedding...

"Well, if you change your mind..."

I nod. "I'll let you know."

"Good. First things first, then, I need to find you something for dinner." Elyse stands and looks over to the corner of the room.

"Excuse me?" My brow wrinkles as I follow her gaze.

"To wear. For your dinner with the Lord."

As she walks toward the wardrobe standing in the corner near the bathroom, I get up out of my chair and follow her. "My what?"

Elyse turns, eyes wide. "I thought he told you. The Lord requests your presence at dinner tonight."

"He didn't mention it," I say, trying to keep the growl out of my voice.

Elyse's cheeks flush, and she opens and closes her

mouth a couple times. "Well, let's see what you have in this wardrobe." She spins away from me and opens the doors, then starts rifling through the items hanging there.

I stop behind her, arms crossed over my chest. Why does Asher want to have dinner with me? It has no relevance to my job duties.

Although, as the thought passes through my head, I realize we haven't established exactly what my employment will involve. A flutter moves up my chest. I'd come here willingly, but it appears more and more that I've become some sort of prisoner.

Not that it matters. I came here to spy. If that means playing the Lord of Night's little games, then so be it.

"What do you think of this?" Elyse asks, turning to show me a red dress.

It's covered in tiny jewels and looks like a cascade of silk and blood. Which Asher would no doubt enjoy.

"Not really…"

She nods, unperturbed, and keeps flipping through the wardrobe. A few moments later she pulls out another and raises her brows in an unspoken question. This one is black and voluminous, with lace along the bodice and sleeves. Beautiful, but far too much… everything.

"Umm…"

A determined look crosses over the Incantrix's face. She bites her lip and dives back into the wardrobe. I try not to stare at her too intensely. The idea of dressing up for Asher makes me want to stab someone.

Which is when a realization hits me.

I may not be able to kill my enemy with magic, but that doesn't mean I can't do it the old-fashioned way: a blade to the heart. If he has one.

Elyse turns a third time. "This?"

Shoving down my thoughts of murder, I look at what she's pulled out of the wardrobe. It's a simple silk sheath dress that flares slightly below the knee, gray-violet depending on the way the light of the lanterns hits the fabric. A shade close to the color of my eyes. It has only tiny sleeves made of gossamer fabric which I know are going to make me feel exposed, but it lacks the lace and beads and excess of the other two.

"I suppose that will work," I say reluctantly.

Elyse beams as if I've spoken the most glowing compliment one could utter. "Great. I'll make sure it fits."

She gestures for me to disrobe, and after I've done so and thrown all my clothing onto the bed, she slides the silky thing over my head. It hugs my body in a way I don't care for at all, but when I voice my complaint, Elyse just makes a *tsk* sound and ignores me.

"It does need to be a bit longer, though," she says.

A hum of magic moves over her, and the fabric at the hem, which falls just above my ankles, extends another several inches until it touches the floor.

"There." She stands back, a satisfied smile on her face. "What do you think?"

She walks me over to the mirror which stands in a wooden frame a couple of feet away. Looking at my reflection, it seems a stranger stares back at me.

"I don't think I've ever worn a dress before." I wrinkle my nose. "Hopefully it will be the last time." When I realize how rude I sound, I stammer, "I mean—no offense."

Elyse laughs. "None taken. Now, about your hair…"

I let her fiddle with my long strands as a thought worms its way into my head. "Elyse?" I ask, meeting her eyes in the reflection of the mirror.

She raises her brows. "Yes?"

"What did… what did the Lord tell everyone about me? About why he brought me here?"

Elyse goes silent for several moments, her hands dropping from my hair and falling still at her sides. "He isn't one who tends to explain his motives for things," she says. "As is appropriate for someone of his stature, of course," she adds hastily.

"Well, but everyone must still be talking. What do they think?"

She doesn't answer, so I turn and face her. "Elyse." Both my tone and my eyes implore her.

The Incantrix fidgets before me. "Dozens of people saw the incident on the bridge in Syreni territory," she begins slowly. "So, that part is fact. What you did… your powers…"

After a moment's pause, she continues. "It makes sense, of course, why the Lord would want someone with magic like yours. But people still talk. The fact that he's keeping you locked away up here, giving you special treatment, that's what people wonder about. What happens between just the two of you."

She blushes. Not that it's anything I couldn't have guessed myself.

"And the dinner. That's not going to help," I say softly.

"No." She shakes her head. "It's just that no one knows your place in things. You're obviously being treated differently than one of the warriors. So, naturally, the generals wonder if he's going to replace one of them."

A shimmer of surprise moves through me. "Generals?"

"There are three," she says, mistaking my question for lack of knowledge, though I already know who the generals are. "So if we have to attack all three houses at once, there will be someone to lead each battle. Though it tends to end up as one to lead the Incantrix, one to lead the fire demons, and one to lead the cold-ones."

It had never occurred to me that I could be placed in command of an army. I shake my head. "He can't possibly be considering that."

Elyse shrugs. "When information is not forthcoming, rumors run wild." She pauses a moment, and then, shyly, says, "So, you don't know his plans yet, either?"

I shake my head. "Haven't the slightest clue."

Her eyes search mine as if trying to determine if I'm being truthful. Then, she turns me back to face the mirror. "I think we should pin your hair up."

"No. The dress is more than enough. I'm a magic wielder, not a lady." I give myself one final look in the mirror. "If he wants me to dine with him, he'll have to take me as I am."

A look of mild shock runs over Elyse's face, but then she smiles. "Okay, then. I guess we're done here." She looks up at the clock on the fireplace mantel. "One of the servants should be here soon to collect you."

I shiver at the word *collect*. As if I'm some sort of specimen.

Elyse walks to the door and I follow. "Thank you," I say before she leaves. "You're the only one here who has been nice to me."

She smiles and dips her head. "I'll try to start my own rumor—that you're humble and not all that scary... even if you do have a great distaste for dresses."

She laughs and I find myself joining her.

"Just joking on that last part. I won't tell a soul," she promises.

I watch her stride down the hall before closing the door behind me and going to sit on the edge of my bed. My stomach churns at the idea of sitting through a dinner with the Lord of Night—Asher. I still don't know the fate of my faction from the battle last night, and he wants to sit around like we're not at war? It's ridiculous and unnecessary. Making me his little pet is just going to make it impossible for me to talk to anyone and do my job. Elyse could prove to be a useful asset in that regard, but if she's the only one, my intel is likely to be very limited.

Guilt washes over me at the idea of using the one person who's shown me kindness. But then I remember another person who'd shown me kindness, taken me under her wing when no one else would. Lyri. Grief replaces the guilt, and then hard resolve replaces the grief. I'm here because of Lyri. And my sister. And because my faction needs me.

There can be no softness in war.

CHAPTER
FIFTEEN
ASHER

I take the usual seat in my dining room, at the head of my somewhat small table by the fireplace. Somewhat small in comparison to the huge tables on the first floor of the palace, where the other Daemonium and Incantrix dine. I always dine here, in this room around the corner from my suite on the second floor. In fact, it's been years since I've shared a meal with someone else.

Which is why it feels utterly strange to be sitting here awaiting my new Incantrix. If Zara can even be called that… she's so different from the others, it seems she barely falls in the same category. A designation I am quite familiar with.

My hunger surges and I take a long drink from my wine glass. I am just setting it back down when she enters the room.

Zara moves toward the table with a lithe stride both graceful and deadly. I can only imagine she's walked that way toward many a foe before they fell to her magic or her blade. Elyse clearly had a hand in the dress she's wearing, though her raven hair cascades over one shoulder, loose and untamed. She meets my eyes for a moment over the table, and her expression burns with something borderlining on defiance.

Her confidence wavers for a brief moment when she reaches the table, as if unsure what to do. One of the servants hurriedly pulls out her chair at the end opposite mine and she folds herself into it. After pouring her some wine, which I'd expressly instructed them not to put blood into, unlike mine, the servant strides away again.

"Thank you for joining me," I say, offering her a small smile.

She blinks, her expression shifting again for a moment. Only about eight feet separate the ends of the table, and I can see the candlelight flickering in her eyes.

"I'll admit, I was surprised by your invitation," Zara says. "Or do you dine with all your new recruits?"

I can tell by the way she says it that she knows I do not. "So, what you're really asking is, why did I bring you here?" A smirk tugs at my lips. She really is refreshingly direct.

She nods slowly.

I lean back in my chair and take another sip of my wine. I'm not wearing my mask tonight. For some reason, with Zara, it feels unnecessary. And not just because she's already seen me without it.

"Well, we haven't talked through the terms of your

employment, have we?" I nod toward her glass. "Don't care for wine?"

"Not particularly." She shrugs.

I cock my head to the side. "The taste or the loss of control?"

"Both, I suppose."

Her eyes lock onto mine for a moment, and I feel that stir of Night spark between us. Across the table, Zara shivers.

"So, terms of employment?" she asks, redirecting the conversation.

"To be entirely honest, I don't yet know what I'm going to do with you," I say. "What I know is that you're too powerful to let out of my sight for long. Too great a liability."

She purses her lips tightly together before speaking. "What exactly does that mean?"

"It means that where I go, you go. Until we figure this out."

"Figure what out?" she growls, leaning forward slightly. Her finger twitches toward the silver butter knife on the table. Someone like her probably *could* make it into a deadly weapon.

I raise a brow. "You know, for someone who came to me seeking a job, you seem oddly obstinate and unhappy receiving any sort of orders. Has anyone ever told you that?"

She takes a visible breath and leans back. "This just

isn't what I had in mind when I came here." She waves her hand around the dining room.

"Well, your entire existence is a surprise to me, so we're far from even."

I pin her in my gaze and another shiver runs over her.

"Everyone is talking," she says, her voice softer now, though still holding a faint growl. "About why I'm here. Staying on the second floor."

"And you really care so much about the opinions of others?" I tap my fingers lightly on the white tablecloth. "I can't imagine this sort of gossip is new for you, possessing talents such as yours."

Her jaw clenches, and I know I've struck a nerve.

"I suppose I'll tell everyone you're my bodyguard." I shrug. "That will explain things."

She snorts. "Like anyone will believe that. You hardly need protection."

"I, unlike you, don't care what they do or don't believe." Another sip of my wine as I watch her.

Two servants appear at the door and with a nod from me, they enter and stride forward, placing small bowls of soup before us. The first of five courses. I don't often partake in real food, so I'm indulging a bit.

After the servants have left and we've both tasted the soup, a creamy potato concoction with herbs and greens, I look up at Zara again.

"Tell me how you came to be here," I ask her. "I want to know how you've been living here in this city, under my nose this whole time, with all that power. With such a strong connection to Night."

She goes still and takes a sip of her water goblet before answering. "My parents died when I was young. We fell in with Factionless rebels to survive. I was in a prison camp for a while, but then I escaped."

"We?"

She'd been looking down at the table, clearly uncomfortable speaking about the past. Now her eyes move to mine, and they burn with a strange intensity.

"My sister. She's dead now."

A strange prickling sensation moves over my skin. "I'm sorry to hear that."

"Casualty of war," she says, and her voice burns with clear hatred.

"And you want to end that war." It's a statement more than a question, because the truth is clear in her body language.

"I told you, I came here to be a part of something that matters." Her fingers grip the edge of the table so tightly that I can see the white of her knuckles. "You're the leader of this cursed city, so…" she trails off, shaking her head.

Hunger lashes through me more strongly than anything I've felt in a long, long time. I clench the fingers of my left hand, which sits on my thigh under the table, so hard that blood wells up. The scent of iron hits my nose and the pain keeps me in check. Keeps me from striding around the table and devouring the woman who sits there.

I'm not sure why she's here. Why she fell, literally, at

my feet and into my life. Someone with a connection to the wild magic nearly as strong as mine, someone who awakens the tiniest glimmer of hope inside me. An emotion that died entirely after the first century of my rule, buried under the weight I carry. The shackles of Night, my prison and my destiny.

The other houses think I maintain control of the city because I'm power hungry. Which once, long ago, was true. But now, if they knew the dark truth, they'd stop this ceaseless, senseless war and realize their pursuit to take the helm is pointless.

If only they knew.

CHAPTER
SIXTEEN
ZARA

I stare at Asher across the table as he seems engaged in some sort of inner battle. What did I say that made him so agitated? Does he somehow know I've left out a vital part of the truth regarding my past? The way he's looking at me makes the hairs stand up at the back of my neck.

Then he visibly relaxes and forces a smile, his predator vibes subsiding.

"I'm glad you think I can make a difference," he says. "Your optimism is… energizing."

I stiffen. "You think me naive?"

He shakes his head, and I can't read the emotion that burns in his eyes. "I think—I think that you coming here changes things. For better or for worse, we have yet to see."

Before I can begin to contemplate a response to such a loaded statement, the servants are back, clearing the soup and replacing it with some sort of delicate salad fancier than anything I've ever eaten. I don't know how I can possibly eat given the company and the conversation, but I'm also not going to let an opportunity like this pass me. The man who will very likely be the death of me sits just feet away. Any day, any hour, any moment could be my last. I'd realized that down in the catacombs today.

"So," Asher says, after taking only a couple bites of food and then setting down his sterling fork. "Tonight, we begin. House Syreni and House Animus have both called for a truce after the battles last night and are prepared to offer retributions for their assassination attempts. Negotiations will be held at midnight, in a neutral location."

I fight to suppress the flicker of emotion that moves through me. All day I've been wondering how my faction fared in the battle last night. It seems Kieran survived, and I feel a swell of relief. The negotiations are not unexpected —it's how things typically go after one of the factions attacks the other—but it hadn't occurred to me that I'd see my commander while in my role as a spy.

"Why do you hold the allegiance ball?" I ask, the question popping out of me before I can decide if it's a good idea. "It always ends like this, doesn't it?"

Asher sighs and sips his wine. "Why indeed…"

I wonder for a moment if I've angered him. He sets down his wine and locks me in his intense gaze, and I feel that tug from Night within my gut.

"I suppose," he says after several long moments, "That if I decide to forgo the allegiance ball, I am giving up on the idea of allegiance altogether. And if I give up on the mere possibility of a united Night, then what's the point of fighting this war at all?"

Confusion flickers through me like the flames of the candles dotting the tabletop. It's not at all the answer I'd expected. "Why not just give the factions their freedom and be done with it?"

Asher makes a strange sound deep in his chest, a velvety rumble, which I realize a moment later is laughter. But it's not mirth, there's a bitter twist to it. "You speak of things far beyond your understanding, shadow wielder."

I frown, crossing my arms over my chest. "Well, why don't you explain it, then? If you can descend to my level."

"Maybe one day I will."

The emotion drops from his face, as if he put on his silver mask. Perhaps that's why he wears it when he ventures beyond his personal quarters. To hide the depth of feeling there. Because he may be a monster, but he's not the sociopath I'd always imagined. It's clear he feels a great many things.

Unease ghosts through my stomach. He's not at all what I was prepared for, which makes this mission a hundred times more deadly.

Abruptly, Asher rises from his chair, setting his cloth napkin down on the table. "I'm afraid I must excuse myself. I need to prepare for the negotiations later tonight."

My eyes follow him as he strides from the room, but he doesn't make eye contact. His huge stride takes him to the door in moments, and as he passes me, I feel the swirl of that shared wild magic between us, electric and hot.

I sit there, staring at the empty doorway long after he's passed, until one of the servants enters and places the main course before me. I try to eat, but after a couple of bites, my stomach churns and I get up from the table myself.

It's clear my words angered the Lord of Night, which is not why I came here. I thought I could do this, thought I could pretend, but I see now how incredibly foolish an idea that was. My rage and my hatred, of both the Lord and this war, bleed through into everything I do. I may be an expert at spying from afar, but this? This insane dance with sure death?

This I cannot do.

At the negotiation tonight, I have to find a way to speak with Kieran privately. Tell him I can't do this. Either I plant a dagger in Asher's heart, or I leave. Because if I stay, it's only a matter of time before my desire for revenge becomes so transparent that I risk not only my life, but my faction.

One way or the other, this ends tonight.

CHAPTER
SEVENTEEN

ASHER

I stride down the hall, away from the dining room, and Zara, and the hunger that threatens to consume me. One of the servants sees me coming toward him and approaches. His eyes blink rapidly and his voice shakes. "My Lord? Do you require something?"

I can hardly blame him, with the magic roiling off me and my inner predator barely contained beneath the surface.

"Send pitchers of wine and blood to my room. Separate pitchers—I will mix them myself."

"Yes, My Lord." He bows and hastens away.

When I get to my room, I slam the door behind me and pace back and forth. I haven't come so close to losing control of my hunger in over a century. It doesn't make sense. I'd consumed all those souls two nights ago at the allegiance ball. I shouldn't need more yet.

Zara. Somehow, she is responsible for this. The correlation is clear, but I don't understand *why*.

We share some kind of bond with the wild magic at the heart of Night, that much is clear. What isn't clear is why that makes me *crave* her with such intensity. It's quite possible she's the answer to my curse, my terrible burden. She could be the key to everything. I need to protect her, not claim her.

What dark corner of my psyche wants to drink from the one person who might be able to save me?

I go still. Perhaps that's just it…as much as I've fought against the darkness within, tried to redeem myself for past sins, maybe the monster I am at my core doesn't want to be saved.

There's a knock at the door, and in my state of agitation I spin, knocking a chair halfway across the room. It clatters noisily against the wall. When I open the door to the poor servant, he's paler than flour. He tries to stammer something, but I just take the silver tray with the two pitchers out of his hands.

"Thank you," I say. I try to sound calm, but there's still a rumble in my voice.

The door shuts behind him and I blur back across the room, setting the pitcher of wine on my bureau. I raise the other pitcher to my lips and drink it down, the whole thing, a rush of crimson. I somehow manage not to make a mess, getting only a drop or two on the collar of my shirt.

The blood is only a temporary fix, something to take the edge off but not something that truly feeds me. It's the magic, the souls, that I really need. A torment I live with every moment of every day because of one terrible choice two centuries ago. I'd let my hunger for power get the better of me. And now all I am is hunger.

I walk across the room and right the chair I'd knocked over, then sit down in it. A glance at the clock on the wall tells me it's two hours until midnight. We'll need to leave for the negotiation in an hour. I can only pray my hunger doesn't return with such intensity before the meeting is concluded.

For a moment, I contemplate leaving Zara behind. Being in her presence is only going to make it worse. But as the thought moves through my mind, I realize the idea of leaving her behind would drive me even more mad. I can't be with her, and I can't be without her.

I should have killed her last night on the bridge.

Now, it's far too late for that, even though I have a feeling deep within my core that she's going to be the end of me.

If I sit here in my room, I'm going to implode. I get out of the chair and head into the suite beyond, feeling the pulse of Zara's magic on the other side of the wall as I stride past. Once in the halls, I head west, continuing until I hit a back stairwell that takes me out to the practice courtyard. From there I travel swiftly through the garden, down the steps that lead beneath the earth, and into the catacombs. When the glow on the far side of the room behind the temple greets me, I immediately feel a sense of calm.

I stay there, beneath the earth, until it's time to leave.

EIGHTEEN

When I climb into the large black carriage, Asher is already waiting there for me. I settle myself on the velvet cushioned bench opposite him, and a moment later he knocks on the window and the driver urges the horses forward.

I've never ridden in a carriage before. It feels oddly intimate being in a small wooden box with someone, in the dark no less. Especially when that someone is the Lord of Night.

"You changed clothes." He gives me a nod, as if in approval.

I look down at my usual attire, boots, jacket, daggers, and all. My brows raise. "Did you expect me to wear the dress to our war negotiations?"

A small smile. "No... I..." The smile drops. "I apologize for my abrupt departure at dinner. Sometimes my nature gets the better of me. My hunger."

I blink and nod. I'm surprised by his candor, and sitting here, knowing he wants to drink from me, is unsettling to say the least. It's yet another thing I never expected coming into this. This connection of both magic and blood. Silence falls between us and I become very aware of the sound of the horses' hoofbeats, the roll of the wheels over the cobblestones, the creak of the carriage shifting back and forth.

"Why do you keep rejecting my offer of a partner to perform rites with?" Asher asks abruptly.

In the darkness, his eyes glitter as he locks gazes with me. The directness of the question sends a shiver of shock along my skin.

"Why do you want to know?"

He makes a small gesture with one hand. "Curiosity, merely. Rites are so commonplace. I just want to know why you don't perform them. Or why you don't want to at the Palace of Night."

I look out the window a moment, my cheeks burning. Moonlight paints the streets silver. I want to summon my shadows and disappear.

"It's difficult to find someone I won't hurt," I say finally. "Someone whose magic is strong enough."

Across from me, Asher goes still. "I see," he says softly. "That would be a challenge indeed. I suppose we all have our prices to pay to wield the magic of Night."

His wistful tone makes me turn back to him, but now he's the one looking out the window of the carriage. I can't imagine what he, the Lord of Night, ruler of this entire city that is the only world we know, must give up. He holds all the power here, and yet he makes it sound like a sacrifice.

The sooner I can claim his life and never have to see his face again, the better.

But before my hatred can get the better of me, the carriage stops and the door opens. Asher gestures for me to get out first, which I do, ignoring the offered hand of the servant outside. A huge stone building rises before us, a house perhaps, or a place of learning. Another carriage already sits outside.

Asher strides ahead of me as we head for the entrance. We pass through into a broad, long hallway lit with candles set in alcoves in the walls. At the end of the passage is a huge, high-ceiling chamber. A large table sits in the middle, square with the center cut out so that there are four distinct sides. An empty fireplace frames one end of the room, and an intricate mural the other. I catch a glimpse of dragons and unicorns in the faded paint before my gaze flicks back to those seated at the table.

I can tell instantly they're Syreni from their bright hair, large eyes, and the spell bubbles around their lower halves which glow aquamarine beneath the table. Lord Octavius sits in the center of his side of the table, a woman on each side of him. Are they advisors or generals? He wears a silver coronet over his golden hair, set with a single sapphire in the center. His metallic tunic is form-fitting and has a texture like fish scales.

"Lord of Night," Octavius says, hovering from his seat slightly and bowing his head.

The two women flanking him do the same, and Asher nods his head to them before walking around to the side of the table closest to the fireplace. I hesitate a moment before following him, but he turns and looks at me over his shoulder, his expression making it clear I should do so. The eyes of the Syreni follow me as I walk behind Asher. When we reach our seats, Asher gestures to the one at his left, which puts me on the side adjacent to them.

There is no small talk as we wait for the others, which is fine by me. Luckily, there is no time for boredom to set in as less than a minute after we sit down, four Angelus enter the room. When they draw close to the table, they all bow and murmur greetings to Asher. Lady Ellielle's gaze burns into me with unveiled curiosity and suspicion. Her pewter wings fold behind her like crossing swords as she takes her seat.

And then the representative of the fourth house enters the room, and my heart climbs into my chest.

Kieran strides across the room, his frenetic dragon energy sending a heat wave across us all. Or maybe I'm the only one who can feel it. His eyes land on mine and flare in shock for a moment. Then he settles himself into the chair directly across the table from me and Asher. He hasn't brought an entourage like the others, it's just him.

"Lord of Night," he says, his voice a soft growl, bowing his head the briefest of moments to Asher.

I feel a flare of magic inside Asher's chest which tugs at me almost physically. The tension between the two of them is palpable. Asher's fingers tighten on the table, and

Kieran's eyes narrow before flicking almost imperceptibly to mine. He's clearly wondering why I'm here. He no doubt hadn't expected me to get *this* close to the Lord of Night.

"Thank you all for coming tonight," Asher says. "I am glad we can put the needs of Night above our differences."

Octavius and Ellielle incline their heads slightly in acknowledgement, but Kieran stares stubbornly ahead, his jaw tight. His gaze flicks to mine again, and beside me I feel Asher's magic roil a second time. It's like a coiled snake, ready to strike. Kieran is going to blow my cover if he doesn't pull it together.

Lady Ellielle provides a much-needed distraction.

"Might I ask, My Lord, who you have brought with you tonight? I do not recognize this new Incantrix of yours."

I stiffen as the gazes of the entire table fixate onto mine.

CHAPTER
NINETEEN

KIERAN

The room goes still as Lady Ellielle's question hangs in the air. Apparently, having not been part of the assassination attempt at the allegiance ball, she feels her head is safely off the chopping block tonight. I'm obviously not the only one wondering why the hell Zara is here, though for very different reasons than everyone else.

The Lord of Night goes still, and power radiates off of him. "I did not realize my choices require any explanation, Lady Ellielle."

His wave of magic strengthens until Ellielle winces. Even feeling only the outer bands of the force he focuses on her, it's all I can do not to flinch under the pressure of it myself.

But then the ruler of the city smiles and releases his vice grip on the room. "I'm happy, however, to introduce my latest recruit. Her name is Zara."

His smile widens, and he offers no further explanation. Which is, of course, quite intentional. Zara sits at his side, stoic as usual, giving no indication that his little power play affected her, physically or otherwise.

"Now that introductions are out of the way, let's start the negotiations." The Lord's eyes shift to Octavius. "The Syreni may put forth their offer."

Offer. Because the negotiations are merely each side serving up retribution for their so-called crimes until our iron-fisted leader is satisfied. My entire life has been consumed by this one man's appetite for power.

Octavius pulls himself up even taller and locks gazes with the Lord of Night. "I am prepared to offer six lives, one to represent each of your attackers, if it pleases you, My Lord."

A ripple of emotion moves over Zara. My eyes flick to hers again. I can read her like a book: she's disgusted that Octavius would offer his people instead of his own life. They were only following their leader's orders, after all. A sentiment I echo myself.

But Octavius is the least of my concerns right now.

I am hugely unsettled by Zara's presence here. I'd expected her to be successful in infiltrating the Palace of Night and making her way into the inner circle of its heartless ruler. Otherwise, I never would have assigned this task to her. But why—and how—is she *here*? It's been a little over a day since she left the Animus. How had she managed to get herself invited to the negotiations in lieu of the Lord's own generals?

There's something about the feel of magic that moves between them that also disturbs me. Something in the way the Lord almost seems to lean toward Zara, as if he can't be parted from her. My inner dragon growls in fury. Zara belongs to *me*—I made her what she is. And I'm beginning to think I've made a massive miscalculation in sending her on this mission.

But before I can get further agitated, the Lord of Night pins me in his bronze gaze.

"And what of House Animus? What do you offer as retribution?"

I take a breath to calm the beast within and make sure my words are even before they part from my lips. "As you know, My Lord, you already claimed the life of the Animus warrior who attacked you."

My eyes scan across the table, from Octavius to Ellielle and back to our ruler.

"But I am always prepared to take full responsibility for the actions of any of my warriors. It's the only honorable thing to do."

Octavius turns a red-cheeked, seething gaze upon me.

"Therefore," I say, "If you must claim a life, mine is the only one fit to claim."

I see Zara stiffen, her gaze locking onto mine. I keep my eyes carefully averted.

The Lord of Night narrows his eyes and another flare of power moves across the room. "I see. You wish death, then?"

"I wish only to pay what I owe. And I defer to your wisdom, as ruler of Night, to claim what you feel is just."

Silence falls as the Lord's eyes burn into mine. After several moments, he finally speaks.

"If I claim your life, then I must also claim Octavius's life."

If I'd thought the Syreni leader looked red before, the shade of scarlet he now turns makes the previous coloration a mere pixie's blush.

"Then I will have two leaderless houses in a city on the brink of chaos with each rise of the sun and moon." The Lord of Night growls and shakes his head. "Octavius, you will give me the life of your head Incantrix. No further sacrifice will be required."

Octavius nods sharply, failing at an attempt to hide the gush of breath he releases. "My Lord shows infinite wisdom. I have her waiting nearby, pending your judgement. She has been under lock and key since the surrender of our forces at the bridge last night. Give me a few minutes, My Lord."

I don't bother hiding the scowl of loathing I direct at Octavius as he gestures to one of his advisors and they float quickly from the room in one of their spell bubbles. Another heavy silence falls as we wait for the sacrificial lamb to return. Time melts slowly as the minutes pass, and I force myself to keep from darting glances at Zara.

What seems an eternity later, the advisor enters the room again, an Incantrix walking ahead of her, chained at the wrists and ankles. The witch keeps her head bowed, resigned to her fate, it seems. The Lord of Night rises from his chair and indicates for the Syreni to line her up against one of the walls.

"What is your name, Incantrix?" the Lord asks, his voice a deep rumble.

The Incantrix finally raises her head, and the look she casts him is pure, scorching hatred. "Selena," she says, spitting the word out as if she could poison him with it. And maybe she could, if he wasn't so powerful.

"Selena, you have been sentenced to death for your role in the attempt on my life," the Lord of Night intones. "Lord Octavius has agreed to this retribution for your crimes."

She says nothing, just continues to glare balefully at him. Her eyes seem to fixate a moment on Zara, too, for some reason.

Without warning, there is a rush of power like all the stars in the sky exploding. Selena doesn't even have time to scream. The Lord of Night rips through her with his magic, yanking her soul from her body and absorbing it into his own. Power shimmers around him like sparks from the sun. Beside him, a shiver moves over Zara, though her face remains impressively impassive.

And then it is done.

I survived. Now I need to figure out how to get Zara away from this man. Tonight.

I stare at the body of the dead Incantrix lying on the floor not a dozen feet away from me. Images of Lyri blink behind my eyelids with violent force. My pulse races hot, I can feel each desperate surge of my heart as if my blood is trying to escape my body.

If I'd succeeded during the battle on the island and brought Selena before Asher as planned, this death would be on my hands. I've taken lives before, and I'd been prepared to take this one. So why does it bother me so much?

Selena had recognized me, of course, from the night before. She'd thought I worked for the Daemonium, and she'd been prophetic, it seems. Had Asher also realized she was the same witch who held a knife to my throat, the one who brought about our fateful meeting?

As if sensing my thoughts, Asher flicks his gaze over to mine, the glow of Selena's soul still fading from his eyes, a pale silver. Some emotion moves over his face, quick and unreadable. I battle to hide whatever expression must be passing over my own features, sucking in a deep breath and clenching my fingers into my palms.

"It's time to go," he says, voice low and terse.

Then he strides across the room, black cloak billowing behind him.

I blink and get out of my chair, following as he exits the room. My eyes dart over to Kieran as I move. I catch up to Asher and we've just reached the candle-lined hallway when a voice rings out behind us. Ellielle.

"My Lord? May I have a word in private?"

Asher spins so quickly I almost run into him. The Angelus is standing in the doorway to the room we'd just left. They eye each other for a moment, then Asher jerks his head in a sharp nod and steps into a smaller chamber off the hallway. Ellielle follows and closes the door behind them.

A moment later the three Syreni float by, the two women carrying Selena's body between them. They make haste in their magical orbs, seeming intent on being gone before Asher comes back out of the room. A wise idea, no doubt.

And then, in a roil of heat and golden eyes, Kieran saunters into the passage. He heads straight for me, the look on his face so intense I back up a couple of steps. He stops a mere inch from my body, a low growl rising from his chest.

"Are you okay? How you did you..." He shakes his

head. "Never mind that." He places his hands around my upper arms and squeezes.

"I can't do what you want me to do," I say in a rush. My eyes dart over his shoulder to the closed door across the hall. "If I stay in the Palace of Night... I just need to leave. As soon as possible."

Kieran lifts a hand to the side of my face and strokes one finger down my cheek. His skin is rough, and it sends a shiver through my belly.

"Agreed. It was a mistake to send you. It's far too dangerous."

I shake my head. "I'm not worried about myself. What I'm saying is that I can't be in his presence another moment without slitting his throat. It's one or the other: I kill him, or I leave."

His free hand slides around the small of my back, pulling me closer. "I just want you to come home."

"Now?"

He nods. "Now."

We turn to make our escape, which is the exact moment the door across the hall starts to open. I have just enough time to take a step back from Kieran before Asher appears. The look they cast each other is enough to melt stone. Ellielle steps out of the room behind Asher and walks quickly down the hall toward the exit. After several tense moments, Kieran gives a small bow and does the same, walking away from me without a backward glance.

My heart climbs into my throat as Asher moves slowly toward me.

"Why was the Lord of Animus speaking to you?" he asks, his tone dark and deadly.

I raise my gaze to Asher, unflinching. If I can't sell this lie, my life is forfeit. "He was trying to find out who I am to you. It seems my appearance created a stir."

Asher's jaw rolls. "Of course he was," he growls. "My brother is always trying to spy on me. When he's not making attempts on my life, that is."

He spins and strides for the street, leaving me standing in the flickering light of the candles as my world turns upside down.

Kieran is the Lord of Night's *brother?*

TWENTY-ONE

ASHER

Zara's face looks ashen as she climbs into the carriage behind me. It begins to move back down the street, and the silence stretches thick between us.

I'm not sure why I told her about my brother. It's something I've kept secret for over two hundred years. We'd parted ways so long ago, and the war claimed so many lives, that there are few who still remember. House Angelus and House Syreni have had countless leaders in that time span, one rising to usurp the one before in an endless cycle of power grabs, so they certainly have no knowledge of it. And Kieran himself has made it clear he wants no ties to his former family. Only a few remain who know the truth, and they do not speak of it.

So why, after all this time, I divulged one of my greatest secrets to someone I barely know is a mystery. What is this Incantrix doing to me?

"You seem to be in shock," I say, watching her face as she stares out the window of the carriage.

"I just… I never imagined," she whispers, turning slowly to meet my gaze. "You're enemies, Daemonium and Animus. You always have been."

"Family can be… complicated."

"But—" she pauses, clearly searching for words. "*How*, exactly?"

I know what she means, despite the vagueness of her question. "Our mother was a dragon, our father a hybrid like I am. Kieran took after her, and I took after our father." It feels as if I've swallowed a heavy stone. I do not like to dwell on the past.

"Is that why you spared him? And took Selena instead?"

Zara's eyes burn into mine, and I don't understand the intensity behind them. Why does she care so much?

"Because of familial sentiment?" I scoff. "That would be awfully foolish of me, considering he tried to have me killed not two nights ago."

My words come out barely above a whisper, the lilt of a question hanging amidst them. Because Zara raises an excellent point: has my judgement been swayed? Am I letting emotion contaminate my actions?

"You know—" I begin, but my words are shattered as the carriage explodes around us.

I feel the magical assault a fraction of a second before it hits, enough time to partially shield myself and Zara, wrapping a barrier of power around us. Wood flies everywhere and one of the horses screams, an unearthly sound. We're blasted across the cobblestones, rolling and tumbling and skidding.

Zara lands on top of me, her cheek bleeding from impact with the street. She rolls to her feet quickly, swaying for only a moment before she regains her balance. I join her a moment later, putting my focus into strengthening the shield around us. A few feet away, the carriage driver lies dead. One of the horses breaks free of its mangled braces and gallops off, the other shies, trapped and frantic, letting out another shrill call into the night.

The warriors appear from the darkness, rushing us all at once.

The first wave attacks with more magic, and based on the different auras I feel, there are Incantrix and Daemonium both. Which means these are Factionless fighters, because my own warriors would certainly never move against me. Beyond those in my line of sight, I sense the energy of many Animus, too, their inner beasts growling for violence. For death.

There are dozens upon dozens of them.

Zara and I turn back-to-back and begin our counterattack. I rip souls from bodies, and Zara lights up the night with a blast of power that breaks like a winter storm over her victims. We knock back the first wave easily, but more keep coming without a break in the onslaught. A ball of fire from one of the Daemonium hits me square in the shoulder. Sizzling heat and pain lance through my chest.

It's been a very long time since anyone has gotten past my defenses.

One of the Animus rushes Zara, a tiger that dodges between the magic-bearers to come in for physical combat. We're both still taking rapid fire from spells. As the creature leaps for her, she wraps shadows around herself and vanishes, reappearing after it moves through the space she'd occupied a moment before. She whips her daggers out and drives them down into the beast's neck, but in its death throws it spins and rakes its claws across her thigh.

Letting out a cry, Zara shoves the body away from her and straightens again, throwing another wave of magic outward at those coming for us. The scent of her blood fills the air, a metallic tang mixing with the heat of our magic. The wild magic of Night, which pulses between us, a tangible, radiant thing.

We fight off another wave, and then another, and then another. We're both bleeding now and tiring from the constant onslaught of magical attacks. And still they keep emerging from the darkness, more and more of them.

"You need to open the door to Night again, Zara," I growl over my shoulder. "Like you did in the catacombs. *All* the way." It's too risky for me to do it myself, the consequences would be dire. I've seen what happens when I lose control.

She doesn't answer for a moment, grunting as she blocks a spell. "I almost died," she gasps in reply.

"That won't happen. I won't let it."

I glance at her sideways and see her barely perceptible

nod. And then I feel it, like the tides retreating before a tsunami. A gathering of such power that it tugs the breath from my lungs. The glowing presence of Night surges beneath our feet, far below in its core, and then the wild magic breaks loose.

First there's a pulse that shakes the cobblestones and rattles the windows, like the outer edges of an explosion. Then a rush of wind like a hurricane, bowling over everyone and everything in a quarter mile radius around us. Zara becomes a vessel of the wild magic, a conduit of the force that is Night.

The attack is over, just like that.

Everyone around us is on the ground, dead or unconscious. The wild magic keeps rushing, ravenous, never satiated. I reach down and grab Zara's hand in mine, winding my fingers through hers. With my other hand, I grab the jeweled amulet at my neck and I force the unruly, raging force to settle.

It bucks against me, and Zara and I both fall to our knees. The wind that rushed out across the streets returns, spinning like a cyclone with us at the eye. Zara's raven hair whips around her, her eyes filled with pain as the magic crushes down on us. It's even stronger than it had been down in the catacombs. Have I made her a promise I can't keep?

As the wind and the magic batter us, I pull Zara closer to me, drawing the magic away from her and into me. I release the amulet and wrap my arm around the small of her back. Our chests and torsos press together, our faces so close I can feel her breath on my cheek. Acting on instinct, I press my lips to hers and I inhale, sucking out the excess magic raging in her core. She stiffens against me, but then the wind dies and the wild magic drops away.

In the sudden stillness of the night, I can hear Zara's heart beating. Her eyes are wide, staring into mine, shock and a turmoil of other emotions running over her face.

And then she loses consciousness.

TWENTY-TWO

T he first thing to hit my senses when I come to is the smell of horse. The next thing is a tingle across my lips. Asher *kissed* me. I can still feel a phantom sensation from where he'd pressed his mouth to mine.

It hadn't been a romantic kiss. He'd done it to siphon out the magic burning through me. It'd been rough and brutal and without emotion. If he hadn't stopped the flood of wild magic, we'd both be dead. He'd saved us. Saved *me*. Yet again.

As my awareness fully returns and the blackness fades away, I can feel something else, too. Asher's arms wrapped around my torso, holding me in front of him on the horse. The flare of heat and magic from his chest pressing into my back. The steady roll of the horse's footfalls.

Somehow sensing that I'm awake, his magic pulsates

139

ever so slightly and a rumble moves through his chest as he squeezes me against him. "Back among the living?" His voice rolls around me like velvet, doing something funny to my stomach.

"Set me down," I snap, struggling against him.

He stiffens and holds me even tighter. "We have to get back to the palace first. It's not safe out here."

I slump against him for a moment until he relaxes his grip and then I call shadows, dropping my physicality for a moment and twisting out of his arms. My feet hit the cobblestones and I stride swiftly away from him. I need a few minutes by myself to sort out everything whirling through my head.

I came here to kill the Lord of Night, who in turn has saved my life twice now. Nothing is as I'd expected it to be, and everything I thought I knew is now in question.

Why hadn't Kieran told me that Asher is his brother?

It makes sense why he wouldn't tell everyone. But *me?* How could he send me here to spy on him, to eventually take his life, and not tell me such vital information?

And then to just abandon me when I told him I needed him, leaving me all alone?

Nothing makes sense anymore.

My breath comes in gasps, my heart racing and my palms itching as I jog through the dark streets. As distracted as I am, buried deep in my thoughts, I hear the footsteps behind me a moment too late.

Asher grabs me and spins me against the wall of the

alleyway I'm passing through. "What are you doing?" he growls, his cinnamon-bronze eyes flashing.

"I need a minute," I snarl back. I struggle against him, but his hands around my forearms are like bands of iron.

"Why?"

"Because I just *do*. We were ambushed. We nearly died." I glare at him. "It's not exactly unreasonable."

"Well, you can have your moment back at the palace."

He turns, still holding one of my arms, and tries to drag me back toward the horse. I plant my feet, adding a push of magic, and slip away in the shadows again. Except this time, I don't jog, I run.

Asher is on me in less than three strides, pinning me against the wall again. Instinct takes over and I thrash against him. I know it's only going to make him angry, but I can't stop myself.

"Zara," he growls. "You are *bleeding*. It is not wise to run from me right now."

He's standing so close that his chest presses into mine, so close I can see the stubble along his jawline glitter in the lamplight. His magic wraps around me, blending with mine. I hate the familiar feeling of it, the *sameness*.

I stare up at him defiantly. "Are you going to feed on me? Consume me, like everyone else?"

"Nothing about you is like everyone else."

His words rumble in his chest, and his eyes burn into mine. Then his gaze drops to my neck, and as if he summons it, my pulse begins to race, my blood moving like sparks beneath my skin. His hands tighten around my wrists where he has them pressed against the wall on each side of me, and he inhales deeply. I become excruciatingly aware of the blood on my cheek, down my left bicep, along my collarbone.

He presses me harder into the wall, bending his lips to my neck. Magic and heat hover between us, his breath moving across my skin, his mouth hovering just shy of contact. I should be terrified. I should loath him. I should feel a lot of things right now. But the magic of Night sparks between us, and I don't feel any of the things I should.

Asher's teeth graze my skin and a shiver moves through my body. A shiver and a small moan, a moan that comes unbidden from within me.

With a final growl, Asher lifts me and slings me over his shoulder, carrying me back to the horse. After a moment to gain my senses since I'm now hanging upside down, I pound on his back with my fists.

"I am *not* your prisoner!" Rage flashes through me. *Dark goddess*, I hate him. I hate him so much.

"You are worse," Asher replies, swinging us up onto the horse. "You work for me. And that makes you *mine*, completely and irreversibly."

"I wasn't trying to escape," I snarl. "I just wanted a moment to think."

He wraps one arm around my torso and I wiggle in his grasp. "How many times do I have to tell you to quit struggling, Zara?"

"If you were going to drink from me you would have done it already," I snap.

His breath is hot in my ear. "Do *not* tempt me further. Be still and be quiet."

He urges the horse forward and we fly down the street. Within a few minutes we gallop into the courtyard of the Palace of Night. When the horse halts, Asher slides down off of it face forward, carrying me with him. "Do not make a scene," he says, his tone tight. "Go clean yourself up. I will need you later."

I spin and stalk away from him. Behind me, I hear him call for one of the servants to summon his generals.

When I reach my room in Asher's suite, I slam the door behind me and stride to the bathroom, running a tub of hot water. I slowly peel my clothing off, uncovering the many gashes where my blood had plastered the fabric to my body. I'm shaking I'm so furious.

I'd planned to get out of here tonight, to either kill the Lord of Night or get as far away from him as possible. But just like that, everything has turned upside down.

And now I'm more tangled in this darkness than I was before.

CHAPTER

TWENTY-THREE

ASHER

"What do we know?"

I stare around the table at my generals. We're seated in the Chamber of Souls in the northwest wing of the palace, so named because one entire wall is hung with silver plaques bearing the names of every warrior, both Daemonium and Incantrix, who has died since the beginning of this unending war. I hold all my strategy meetings here because the weight of those deaths reminds me why I bear the burden I bear. It hurts in a way that prevents me from growing numb to it.

"Word is scarce so far among the Factionless, My Lord," begins Helios. His pale skin and gold-white hair make him look more statue than flesh-and-blood.

I lean forward, magic rocketing off of me. It shakes the table and the walls. "That is not what I want to hear."

Malara, my Incantrix general, stares at me unflinchingly, arms folded over her chest. "Just because you don't want to hear it, My Lord, doesn't make it less true. All of our spies are on the task, but it's going to take some time."

"And you, Carcas? Do you have news to share?" I growl to the third and last general.

Carcas shakes her horned head back and forth. "Not much about your attackers. You didn't leave many survivors. But witnesses that live in the area saw some escape, and they're saying that your new Incantrix saved your life. That story is spreading rapidly."

I go still. This makes things even worse. Not only does it reveal my new secret weapon, but it paints a target on Zara's back. Just like the one I've carried for more than two centuries. With a snarl, I clench and unclench my fists on the table. It takes everything within me not to break the whole thing in two.

"There's something else, My Lord." Malara darts her gaze to the other two, and then to me.

"What is it?"

"Well, Zara was herself Factionless, didn't you say?" She pauses. "Has it occurred to you that she's a part of all this?"

The table does creak beneath my fists this time, so hard am I pressing into it. "Of course it's occurred to me, General. Though it seems strange that she'd fight by my side and nearly die herself if she was working for the enemy."

"It's our job to explore all possibilities, My Lord,"

Helios says, his lips stretched thin across his face, giving him a skeletal appearance.

"We can use this to our advantage," Carcas says. "Send Zara to spy. She'll have a better chance getting in with the Factionless than any of our usual spies."

"I need Zara with me," I say, the words rumbling a warning.

"Consider it, My Lord," Malara presses. "We could gain invaluable intel, plus it will dispel some of the... rumors."

"I don't care about the rumors." I glare around the table. "The important thing is finding out who led this attack and squelching it. Three houses fighting against us is enough. We cannot afford for the Factionless to join together against us, too. I can only imagine how many there are, after all this time..."

I should have weeded them out, ripped them up like dandelions in the tulips before they could take hold. If I'm being honest, it had been softness that made me turn a blind eye. I'd secretly admired the ones brave enough to risk death to escape their position in life. They'd found freedom where none had in this city. Least of all me.

And now, that freedom may just be my downfall.

"There is something else," I say. "Lady Ellielle pulled me aside after the negotiation tonight. She says they've designed a powerful weapon that could end the war once and for all. She wants to share it with us, to create a permanent partnership."

Carcas pins me with her yellow eyes. "Why would she need us? If it's so powerful?"

"What does she *want* is more like it," Helios says in his waspy voice.

I shrug. "She would not say. She wants me to see it first before we enter into bargaining."

"You'll need a large envoy for protection," Malara says.

"Of course." I can't take two steps outside these palace walls without someone trying to kill me.

"I'll make the arrangements," Helios adds. "When would you like to go?"

"Tomorrow morning." I swing my gaze across them. "With the Factionless planning goddess knows what, if there is some validity to Ellielle's offer, we need it sooner rather than later."

I should bring Zara with me to Angelus territory. But, as much as I hate the idea, I can't deny what my three closest advisors have suggested... she may be our best chance of getting intel from the Factionless. My eyes rove over them once again. The four of us have fought side-by-side in this battle for over a century and a half. They're as tired as I am.

Things are changing, however, things that have not shifted in a very long time. The wheels on which we've spun for so long, round and round in an unending cycle, are wobbling on their axis. Zara's arrival announced it, and this uprising from the Factionless, along with Ellielle's unexpected offer, all signal an end. I can feel it in the heart of Night, too. A stirring in the wild magic.

Hope is too strong a word for what I feel... too dangerous a word. But for the first time in as long as I can remember, I know, deep within, that things will never be the same again.

TWENTY-FOUR
ZARA

I'm sitting in a tub turned pink with my own blood when Elyse walks in.

"Oh!" she gasps, her hands flying to her mouth.

After a moment to recover she strides over, eyes wandering over the multitude of injuries. I've got a nasty gash in my side from being thrown from the carriage. Plus the place where the tiger sunk its claws into my leg, a scrape along my cheek and collarbone and chest, and an assortment of other smaller injuries caused by blasts of magic.

"I came as soon as I heard," she whispers, shaking her head back and forth. Her eyes are wide and glassy with tears. "The Factionless have never done anything like this. I don't think any of us thought they could."

"Those that are forgotten can be very dangerous," I murmur, hugging my knees to my chest.

"Who's their leader? I never even thought there was one before tonight."

She's right. A coordinated attack like this must have taken extensive planning. "The Factionless don't have a leader. At least, they didn't have one in the past. It goes against the whole purpose of being Factionless."

Her voice drops several octaves as if she's telling a dirty secret. "Back when you were one of them?"

I nod. She, of course, doesn't know I haven't been one of the Factionless since I was a child. But since everyone thinks that's where I came from, I'll of course let them continue thinking that.

Who *had* brought them all together for the attack? While it's been over a decade since my time running in those circles, I've been a spy for almost as many years, so I'm not exactly a stranger, either. How is it that news of this hadn't reached me? The whole thing sits like acid in my stomach. Something isn't adding up.

My bath water is starting to get cold, and when I shift my weight to get up, Elyse helps me stand and then hands me a towel. "I'll go find a healer," she says.

"I just need some salve," I say with a shrug.

She shakes her head. "Some of those look deep. I'm not taking no for an answer, Zara."

Her lips pressed into a firm line, she steers me by the elbow to the nearest chair and shoots me a threatening look before exiting the room. I sit there for a moment, towel wrapped around me, wondering how long I'm going to have to wait here before she gets back. We've been back from the battle for nearly an hour, and it's got to be more than halfway to dawn by this point. I'm hungry and exhausted, and all I want to do is collapse into my bed.

So much has happened since I arrived at the Palace of Night... it seems a lifetime. The duel in the catacombs, discovering the connection to Night that I share with Asher. The dinner, the negotiation, the attack. Not to mention finding out Kieran has been withholding vital information from me.

Somehow, his betrayal is the thing that shatters me most.

My thoughts drift back a few years to a night like this one, unending and fraught with danger. The Animus had been battling all night with the Angelus. I don't even remember why... after a time, most of the battles blur together. I only remember that it was nearly dawn after a night filled with fire and magic and wings against midnight skies... wings of angel and dragon both.

I'd stood on one of the battlements at the edge of our sector, bending shadows and hurling magic at our enemies. But even with all my magic, and my strange connection to Night, the one thing I cannot do is fly. All day and all night my heart had been in my mouth, watching for Kieran, praying to the goddess that he'd return.

And he had, in that final hour before dawn. Bleeding from multiple wounds and clutching one wing to his side, he'd crash-landed a few feet away from me. After he shifted back into human form, I'd helped him hobble to the shelter of a nearby tower so I could heal his wounds.

I'd realized that day that my childhood infatuation had morphed into something much stronger.

As we huddled in the shadows of the tower, I closed wound after wound, my hands trembling as they hovered over him, adrenaline spiking through my veins. Kieran was half-delirious, at times his eyelids fluttering as he moved in and out of consciousness. When I'd finished healing him and leaned back, he'd grabbed my hand.

"Don't go, Zara," he murmured, pulling my hand to his chest. His eyes locked onto mine with feverish intensity. "You're going to end this war one day. You know that don't you?"

I nodded, because I wasn't sure what else to do.

"I believe…" He coughed, wincing at his sore ribs. "The goddess sent you here. To me. I don't want anyone else by my side…"

And then he'd lost consciousness.

The memory tastes like ashes in my mouth now. I'd devoted my entire adult life to Kieran, had been loyal in every possible way. I'd thought he trusted me. But he hadn't trusted me with the plan at the allegiance ball. And he hadn't told me that Asher is his brother. All these years, all these battles. What information does he possess that could have given us the advantage, had we known? He'd sent me into the Palace of Night, risking my life in the process, when all this time he had critical knowledge that could help me?

I don't know what's real anymore.

In my agitation I get up to pace, flinching as my body

turns to one massive point of pain. As much as I loathe to admit it, Elyse is probably right about the healer. The wound at my side and the claw marks are beginning to throb painfully. I could heal myself, but it's much slower and harder on your own wounds because you're recycling your own energy. Carefully, I walk to the full-length mirror, tossing the towel over the chair as I go. My eyes wander up and down my skin. I have so many bloody marks, I look like I was attacked by a pack of wolves.

There's a knock on my door. Elyse must have been fast…

I turn from the glass, striding toward where I left my towel, but the door is already opening. And it's not the healer. It's Asher.

We both freeze.

Those molten metal eyes span the length of my body, and he lets out a low growl. I can't tell if it's anger, because I got so beaten up in the battle, or something else entirely. His predator's gaze sends my heart racing up my throat. I hold very still as he stalks across the room toward me, lithe and dangerous.

Asher stops a foot in front of me. "I require you," he says, his voice flames and obsidian.

My heart pounds even faster, and his eyes flick to the pulse in my neck.

"But first, you need to be healed. Your injuries are too extensive."

"Elyse is on her way to get the healer," I say, finally finding my tongue.

"I will handle that."

Magic swirls in Asher's core, spiraling around us. As I feel his power wash over me, I see flashes in my head of Selena falling prey to him, and Lyri before that. Healing is a different form of magic than others. It's different than our auras merging, it involves taking someone else's magic inside of you. Panic wheels in my chest like a flock of birds and I take a step back.

"I'd rather wait." His eyes flare, so I add, "You lost a lot of blood and magic, too. No need to weaken yourself further."

"I'll decide that for myself," he says, eyes narrowing.

He takes another step forward, hand outstretched over the cut along my cheekbone. I flinch away from him. I can't help it. All I can imagine is someone else's stolen soul blending with mine.

"You think I'm going to hurt you?"

His voice is so low it vibrates along my skin, making me shiver. His eyes burn into me. I shake my head.

"What then?" It's a command, an utterance I cannot disobey.

"Your magic is mixed with... *theirs*," I say, forcing myself to meet his gaze. If he's going to demand the truth, I'm not going to sugarcoat it for him.

"I see," he says. His jaw clenches and the muscles in his cheek roll. For a moment, I'm not sure what he's going to do, but then he says, "Put on some clothes and follow me."

I don't dare to ask questions, not after walking a

knife's edge with him tonight. Asher stalks to the other side of the room and begins pacing impatiently, so I grab a long velvet cloak from the wardrobe and wrap it around me, held in place by one of my leather belts. When he sees me approaching, he turns without a word, knowing I will follow.

We head across the palace, which is eerily dark and quiet at this time of night, so close to dawn. Asher leads us down to the ground floor and out into the practice court-yard. Then beyond, to the walled garden and the entry to the catacombs.

Like the time before, I wonder fleetingly if I am being led to my death.

Down, down, down the steps beneath the earth we go. The scent of bones and magic hits my nose. Then I see the glow, blossoming in the darkness long before we reach the bottom. Only then does Asher turn to look at me, just for a moment, before leading me behind the temple.

When I see the source of the white glow, I stop and stare in amazement for a moment.

It's a subterranean garden of flowering vines. The leaves growing along them are a bright spring green, it's the flowers that emit the light. Voluptuous white petals unfurl from a tiny golden center. They shiver and stir as if in an invisible breeze. I can feel the hairs on the back of my neck rise to attention.

"What is this place?" I finally whisper after staring for quite some time.

Asher pivots his body so he's facing me. In the light

from the vining flowers, his eyes glow silver. "You think me cruel," he says softly. "Power hungry. A murderer."

I go still, and a small, sad smile crosses his lips.

"I was once all of those things. I still am now, but for different reasons. It's time you knew those reasons."

He turns and begins to walk toward the flowers. When he reaches the edge, just before his boots touch the glowing petals, he looks back.

"It all began over two hundred years ago, when my brother and I were new in the world. Before I knew the cost of power."

Asher takes another step forward, one foot after the other, carefully moving between the blossoms. The garden flashes, the glow intensifying until I can't see for a moment. I cover my eyes from the blinding light.

When it fades, Asher is gone, another figure in his place.

TWENTY-FIVE

The memory rises around me, and I wonder for a moment if Zara will be able to see it. I've never shown this place to anyone, so it's possible the magic will not work with someone else. But when I hear a small gasp escape her throat, I know she can see what I do.

I see the memory as if it's a stage play and I am off in the distance, the audience to my own performance. I see *me*, from two hundred years before, young and impetuous and craven for power more than anything else. I also see Kieran, flashes of us together, both competing to wield the greatest amount of magic. Enemies even then, though we didn't fully realize it yet.

We perform spells and rituals and sacrifices to obtain more and more magic, more and more power. Never enough power. We can feel the wild magic that runs through our city, and we want to control it, possess it, all for ourselves. Our father has yet to name his successor as ruler of the Daemonium, and we know that whoever can summon the most magic will take the helm.

And then comes the day that everything changes. I remember every moment, every excruciating detail, and so the memory is painted in the same vividness, here in this magical place, hovering in the air between me and Zara. A crisp winter morning, the sky a perfect seashell blue. Glints of sun coming in through the gray satin curtains in my study. My eyes bloodshot from staying up all night summoning magic. I can even smell the flame and the sulfur from my spells.

Maybe it was because I was so bleary-eyed, having been awake for more than thirty hours, that I lost control. It happens slowly in my memory, though in reality it had been quick as a snake striking. I summon magic, calling it forcefully, speaking the words of an ancient spell I'd found in my texts. Offering myself to it, to power, to hunger.

I offered, and it claimed me. Fully and completely.

The wild magic broke loose from wherever it had been trapped. I hadn't realized until that moment that it *had* been trapped, that there was a great excess of it, waiting for release. From where it came, I still don't fully know. It rushed into me, burning through me like a solar flare, agonizing and endless. Then it ripped through the city, leveling buildings, devouring people whole. It surged out and it created the Waste beyond.

In my desperation to stop it, I'd trapped some of it within my amulet. Satiated for the moment, having destroyed the city and claimed untold lives, the wild magic settled.

Briefly.

I'd soon learned, that same day, that I'd become the anchor for this wild force, its conduit. And with that heavy burden, my natural hunger for blood increased a hundred-fold. To have enough strength to keep the magic contained, both within me and within the amulet, I'd drained count-less more bodies. It still hadn't been enough. That's when I learned that devouring souls was the only thing that gave me enough strength to keep the wild magic in check. Some lives must be sacrificed, or else they all are lost. I was, and am, two hundred years later, the only thing standing between the wild magic and all who live here within the borders of Night. Even now, to this day, if I lose control the wild magic burns through the city, devouring those in its path.

It's my greatest secret, the dark truth of my power. The burden I carry each and every day.

As the memory fades, I meet Zara's eyes over the glow of the flowers. She's staring at me in horror.

I speak softly, afraid I'll startle her. "Have you ever regretted one moment in your life so completely that you'd do anything to change it? Anything at all?"

She doesn't say anything for several long moments, but then she nods.

"That's what this place shows you," I say. "The memory you wish you could change more than anything."

Her eyes, which had been staring in an unfocused way

past my shoulder, hook onto mine. "It was you who created the Waste. Cut us off from the rest of the world."

I nod wearily. "Yes."

"And the war—"

"*That* was not my doing. The battle between the four factions had been raging long before I was born." I sigh and my shoulders slump. "But what the wild magic did to the city—what *I* did—it put me in the position I'm in today. Because my father was one of the victims that first day, when the wild magic ran rampant. Everyone was terrified of what I possessed. And so, I claimed the title Lord of Night, and declared myself ruler of the city and all its factions. I thought it would end the war, but after a time, it only made it worse."

Zara fidgets, shifting her weight as if considering bolting for the stairs. "Why did you show me this?"

I open and close my mouth a couple of times, trying to find the right words. Now that it's come down to it, I feel like I've only added more nails to my coffin.

"I want you to understand," I say, my eyes pleading with her. "I don't claim souls because I want to. I claim them because I *must*. Because if I lose control, it means the end of Night."

She shakes her head. "But it's that way because of *your* actions."

"And I've had more than two hundred years to carry the weight of my selfishness. My greed."

I take a step toward her, but she shrinks back.

"I would give it all up if I could. I want nothing more

162

than to be rid of this power that flows through me." I suck in a shaky breath. "The other factions wish to take it. They have no idea the cost. They think I hoard it because I don't want to give up my throne."

"And there's not even a small part of you that wants to be ruler? To keep the city in your thrall?" Her eyes burn into me, her arms wrapped around her torso as if she's trying to hold herself together.

I shake my head. "It took a century, but that desire has long since faded. If I could safely relinquish it, I would."

Zara's eyes suddenly widen. "You think I can...you want me to..."

I raise a hand to placate her. "I don't know what your existence means," I say softly. "I just know you're the first person in these past two centuries that Night has chosen, as it chose me."

The air between us feels charged, electric. I take a step toward Zara, and this time, she doesn't flinch away from me. Our gazes stay locked together as I approach. When I'm a foot away, our magic sparks between us like heat lightning, flickering in shades of violet.

"Surely you have something you regret," I ask. "A moment you'd do anything to erase?"

She nods. "I used to have a sister, Jaylen. We were separated in the prison camp." Her fists clench and unclench at her sides, and her jaw rolls. "And I told myself that one day I would make it right."

We stare at each other for several long moments.

"You can help me end all of this." I reach out and wrap

my fingers around hers. "I don't know how yet, but I know we can change things."

Zara looks up at me. "Do I have a choice? Or is my fate sealed?" she whispers.

I look into her eyes, feel her warm breath on my face. I realize, with a rumble of heat from the demon side within me, that it's not just our connection to the wild magic that ties us together. The idea of Zara walking out of my life is untenable. It's been such a short time since I found her on that bridge, but I am drawn to her in a way that I haven't felt with anyone else, not in all my many years of existence.

But we can't end this war if we're enemies. Even if there is a dark part of me that wants to keep her by my side, no matter the cost.

"If you want to leave," I say, letting her fingers slide out of my hand, "I won't stop you."

Zara stares up at me for several long moments, then she turns and strides from the catacombs without a backward glance.

CHAPTER
TWENTY-SIX

ZARA

My heart races as I walk up the steps of the catacombs, out through the walled garden, and across the training courtyard. I don't go back upstairs to my room, even though I'm still wearing only a robe. I can find new clothing elsewhere. I head straight through the main courtyard, and the guards do not stop me as I leave through the ornate faded gold gates and travel out into the streets beyond.

I don't know what to make of the emotions swirling through me.

And I certainly don't know where to go from here.

Just hours before, I'd wanted nothing more than to leave the Palace of Night and the man responsible for all the pain and suffering in my life. Somehow, in the span of time since we got into that carriage to travel to the negotiation, everything I thought I knew had been flipped upside down.

Kieran lied to me, has been lying to me this whole time, and then left me there with the most dangerous man alive. I don't know how I can return to him now, return to my home.

Asher, on the other hand…I hate him still. How could I not? He killed my sister and my best friend both. He showed me his past, how his greed and hunger destroyed this city and made our never-ending war even worse.

Why had he shown me his darkest memories?

It wasn't just images I'd seen, clear as day, as if I'd been there. I'd felt his emotions as I saw them, felt his regret and despair. He really thinks I can help him somehow release the wild magic back to where it once was. Get it back into control. And if we can do that, we can stop the needless deaths that occur when Asher loses his grip on the magic, or when the residents of Night try to tap into a source too vast for them to control.

I have a chance to save this city, but that means working with the person I hate most in the world.

Because I *do* hate him. I do. If he thought showing me his past would change things, would make me view him differently, he is quite mistaken.

If I choose to go back, to find a way to control the wild magic and end this war, that doesn't mean I have to give up my revenge. I can still have my justice afterwards, when all of this is over.

The Lord of Night will still pay for his crimes.

An hour later, when the first dove-gray edge of dawn lightens the horizon, I shove my thoughts aside and get up from the church steps I've been sitting on. My feet carry me of their own accord back west, back toward the Palace of Night. Once inside, I head to the second floor, to Asher's suite. I knock on the door to his bedroom, my heart racing once again, my blood spiking fast and hot in my veins.

After a few moments, he opens the door, his eyes flickering with some emotion that passes too quickly to read. He's wearing loose black silken pants and nothing else. My eyes move up the expanse of his chest, criss-crossed with scars over hard muscle, and land on the raw, red flesh along his shoulder where he'd been injured in the attack. There's another gash above the opposite hip.

I can't walk away from whatever this is that lies between us. This joint connection to Night, and all it could mean for the citizens of this place, a possibility to end the war once and for all. I wish I could fight it. I wish I could be selfish. But the pull of the wild magic connecting us is too strong.

"You didn't tell me you were injured, too," I say.

"My injuries are minor." Asher's eyes travel over my robe. "Yours are a distraction."

My breath catches in my chest and my heartbeat spikes, and I know he can sense it by the small rumble of a growl in his core.

"Fine." I cross my arms over my chest, trying to hide my reaction to that sound, the way my nipples harden, very much against my will. "You can heal mine if I can heal yours."

He doesn't respond verbally, just reaches out slowly and slides my robe off one shoulder, exposing the full length of the wound along my collarbone. Magic flares around us, and I bite my lip as I feel his power enter the wound, closing it up and tickling along the edges. It's a mix of pain along with a radiant warmth that feels…quite the opposite.

When the first wound closes, Asher shifts his hand to a scrape along my neck, but I take it and put it down by his side. Then I raise my own hand to his shoulder, hovering my fingers a couple inches above the skin. The wild magic flows through me, knitting together skin and the layers beneath. I ignore the weight of Asher's eyes on mine as my power bleeds into him. He has many old scars on his chest, and as I lower my hand, my fingers graze over a particularly dark one that sits right above his heart.

My eyes finally meet his. I can see the dark hunger there, feel the roil of both his demon fire, and the side that craves my blood. He waits for me to slowly open my robe so he can access my other injuries. Had I performed rites regularly like the other warriors, no doubt this wouldn't feel so intimate, I wouldn't feel so exposed.

Carefully, meticulously, he weaves my skin back together with his magic, starting at the slashes on my thigh and working his way up. I pause him when the sensations of the healing magic become too much and I focus on healing his wounds, though he has fewer to heal. Finally, there is just the one on my cheekbone left, and Asher holds his fingertips above it, his hand almost cupping my face but not quite. His heat and his magic burn into me.

As the sensitive skin below my eye begins to knit back together, I close my eyes and focus on my breathing. Asher is standing so close I can feel the light brush of his hip against mine through our sheer clothing. As the magic moves into me, a ripple of pleasure shivers through my core, and a little sigh escapes my lips. The wound closes, and Asher's palm brushes against my cheek. I open my eyes and our gazes lock together like magnets. He brushes his thumb slowly along my cheekbone where the cut had been, and then, even slower, down across my lips.

I *hate* him. I hate him so much, even more now that I know him, the object of my vengeance, my purpose and my every waking thought.

I hate the wild magic even more for connecting us in this way, for making me feel things I don't want to feel.

But most of all, I hate myself for coming back here. I will *not* succumb to this, whatever this is. The wild magic will not control me as it controls him. Night will not take this from me.

"No more distractions," I murmur, stepping away from him.

Asher's hand falls from my cheek and down to his side, and the sudden lack of his heat and his magic feels like a cold wind sweeping in around me.

"Get some rest," he says, his voice a low rumble in his chest. "Then we have work to do."

I nod and make my way from his room over to mine.

My heart races as I slip beneath the silky sheets. I can feel the bright pulse of Asher's magic on the other side of the suite, impossible to ignore.

Nothing makes sense anymore. The last decade of planning and practice has all been washed away by this... whatever *this* is.

All I know is that tomorrow, everything changes.

CHAPTER
TWENTY-SEVEN
ASHER

I do not sleep while I wait for Zara to awaken. I couldn't possibly after what transpired between us. She'd come back to me. And then the way we'd shared magic...

It seems fate brought us together, though I don't know what any of it means. Have I finally, after two centuries, atoned for what I brought into this world, what I did to this city and its people? I don't feel like I could ever erase that dark mark on my past, but Zara seems a blessing from the goddess. Not only because of her connection to Night and this chance to finally mend things, but because of our connection to each other.

I know she feels something, too, though she's clearly fighting it. Why did she really come here, after being Factionless all her life? How is it she just walked into my life, the answer to all my desperate desires in the dark of night?

Trusting someone else doesn't come easily to me. I'd learned long ago that the closer you let someone in, the easier it is for them to stab you in the heart. Metaphorically and literally.

After I'd unleashed the wild magic all those years ago and become the conduit of Night, Kieran turned on me, claiming I'd murdered our father. Which, in a way, was true. Though completely unintentional, as were all the other deaths caused by the magic ripping through me.

There had only been three great houses then. Those who shifted into animals belonged to House Daemonium, along with the blood drinkers and the fire demons. But even before that terrible day, Kieran had been driving a wedge between the dragons and the demons. Our mother died when we were young, and it started then, perhaps because Kieran felt alone, the odd one out, since my father and I shared the same hybrid demon traits.

So, the day I lost my sovereignty and my father both, I also lost my brother.

He formed House Animus and took all the shifters with him. A month later they attacked, and it was during that battle my brother tried to kill me for the first time. A dagger to the heart, just a centimeter short of its intended target. Night had saved me that day, and every day since. Because it certainly wouldn't be the last time my kin made an attempt on my life.

Kieran had also been the one to convince the other faction leaders that I was intentionally hoarding the magic and causing mass deaths to keep the citizens of Night in line. Ever since, they've been convinced that killing me will grant all of my power to the one who takes my life. He could be right...but he could also be very, *very* wrong. Releasing all that wild magic back into Night... I don't know what would happen.

I just know that I'm so, so tired of this war.

Which is why the hope Zara stirs in me causes an almost physical pain.

My thoughts spin through the past while I wait for her. A few hours later, I feel the slight surge of energy when she awakens, and I go out to the sitting room by the fire so we can discuss our strategy. She emerges from her room a few minutes later and comes to sit across from me in one of the winged back chairs.

"What's your plan?" She asks quietly by way of greeting. Her expression shows no indication of a change in feelings after what transpired earlier. "What do you need me to do?"

I lean forward slightly in my chair. I've tossed the options over in my head the last few hours, and I know what needs to happen, though I loathe being apart from her. "I need someone to get information from the Faction-less. Find out who planned the attack and what their end goal is. How many of them there are."

Zara nods. "I can do that."

"I'll be visiting Angelus territory today," I say. "The Lady Ellielle has a proposition for us."

Zara arches her brows but says nothing. "I'll leave right away, then."

When she gets out of her chair and turns to go, I add, "Use caution, Zara. Word is spreading through the city: who you are and who you're working for."

The slightest ghost of a smile crosses her lips. "I'll manage." She continues across the room, and when she reaches the door, she looks over her shoulder. "Watch out for the angels."

Then she is gone, out into the streets of Night, which have never been more dangerous. I shake my head. She can handle herself. And as she said, I have the Angelus to contend with.

TWENTY-EIGHT

ZARA

B efore I leave, I head to the kitchen to grab breakfast on the go. My stomach is growling angrily after depleting so much magic the night before. It seems absurd that my body can be so demanding about mundane needs when I'm tasked with finding out what kind of rebellion we're dealing with. But it'll be only a moment, and then I can be on my way.

There are a handful of staff down there, and I soon have two pieces of bread and meat to take on the road. As I walk back across the huge room, I go over a plan in my head. I'll go to the tavern first, of course. Find out what Siduri knows of the attack and the rebels. And despite my blithe words to Asher, he's right: I need to watch myself. The very fact that I knew nothing of this attack means things have shifted in Night, and my place in it is not what I thought it was.

A knot forms in my stomach as my thoughts churn. I should be joining the rebels, not gaining intel to use against them. I was born Factionless. Had I not been beholden to Kieran all these years, no doubt I would have been part of this rebellion. It's the first major interruption in this endless pattern we've all been stuck in, year in and year out. On the one hand, the Factionless nearly killed me during the attack. I can't help, however, but admire the way they'd pulled it off.

The bread I'm chewing sticks in my throat as I realize how truly afloat I am. Do I really not consider myself part of the Animus faction any longer? I'm not one of the Daemonium, either. I belong to no one, to nothing. Ironically, it's the cover story I'd given Asher, and now it's come true. A shiver moves across my skin.

I've just reached the door when Tryn enters the room, followed by a half dozen other Daemonium. I haven't seen her since the day I was combat tested in the courtyard, which seems a lifetime ago. Her head turns in my direction and her red eyes lock onto mine as a cold smile turns her lips.

"How is our new recruit?" she calls, blocking my exit. She moves sinuously, serpent-like, as she steps toward me.

"Busy," I respond.

The demons fan out around me, dogs on the hunt. Pack mentality without so much as a spoken word between them.

"I'm on assignment for the Lord of Night," I say. "And I don't think he much cares for being kept waiting."

Tryn flashes me a blade-edged smile. "Our Lord just left in his carriage to travel to Angelus territory. He won't be back until late tonight, I'd imagine."

I don't respond, my eyes flicking across them all, sizing them up. Two of Tryn's companions are the same demons who fought me in the courtyard.

"How is it, sleeping in the personal quarters of the ruler of the city?" asks one of the other Daemonium, a creature with silver wings and solid black eyes.

"Funny you receive such special treatment," says another, "When the Lord has plenty of spies and warriors already."

Tryn's smile turns wicked. "There must be something *extra* you provide him."

"There is, in fact." I let my magic flare out around me. A violet glow sparks at my fingertips as the wild magic moves through me. "Would you care to see it?"

Laughter spikes the air as Tryn steps back and gestures for me to pass. "I'm sure it's very impressive."

I step between the Daemonium, my senses alert to any attack. Then I stride away from them without a backward glance.

When I'm a few paces away, Tryn calls, "Do make sure you're back tonight when our Lord returns. No doubt he'll require those special talents of yours."

I keep my emotions carefully in check as I leave the Palace of Night, calling shadows around me as soon as I hit the courtyard. Not because the guards will stop me but because I don't want to be seen right now. Don't want to think about how angry I am. I'd known the rumors, Elyse had told me as much before. They hadn't bothered me as much then.

But now…

Memories of the early hours at dawn slide behind my eyes. That jump in my heartrate as I knocked on Asher's door. His fingers on my skin as he slid my robe down. The ripples of pleasure his magic sent through me, not just healing my wounds, but spiraling through other places, too.

All my life, I'd viewed the wild magic as a friend. Not a comfy, safe friend, more like a wild animal I'd tamed, a mutual respect. But now it has turned on me, just like Kieran. Now I have this connection to my enemy that grows stronger and stronger. It's like the harder I fight against it, the more inevitable it becomes.

I don't care what fate wants, what Night wants. I will *not* let the rumors be true.

Part of me wishes Tryn had jumped me down there in the kitchen. She's clearly spoiling for a fight. It was just words today, but it's building to something more. I could tell by the way they surrounded me like wolves, the hatred in their eyes. Why they're jealous of my status, I don't know. Who could possibly want to receive the level of attention and scrutiny Asher places on me?

As I travel south toward the tavern, a wintry breeze sweeps down from above. The sky overhead is invisible behind a pale pewter stretch of flat clouds. It's late morning, but I can't tell where the sun is, what with the Waste and the gloomy sky both. I pass an abandoned park, the ground flaming red with fallen leaves. The remains of a stone fountain can be seen within, waterless and cracked, the angel at the center holding a trumpet that has fissures running the length of it. The angel's face is half shorn off from wind and time. Or maybe from that day long ago when wild magic burned through the city. So much about this place makes sense now that I've seen Asher's memories.

This morning I'd been weak. I hadn't fought hard enough against the magnetic pull stretching between me and Asher, a pull I can feel even now, growing stronger the further apart we are from each other. I grind my teeth together and let out a growl, and beneath me, Night responds with a faint pulse of magic.

I hadn't had any sleep when I went to his room this morning, and I was still weak from the attack and all my wounds. But I'm healed now, and I can fight. I can walk away from this. From *him*.

When the tavern rises before me, I realize I've traveled the last few miles completely lost in my thoughts. It's quiet outside, no rowdy calls or music tumbling out into the street. The cold wind whips down again, flinging my hair out behind me, and I pull my jacket more tightly closed. Warm light glows through the windows like squares of pale butter.

"You're alive," Siduri says as I slide onto a barstool a couple minutes later.

I've never been here when she is not working, day or night.

I cock my head to the side. "Is that in reference to the last mission we spoke about, or the attack last night?"

I'm the only one sitting at the bar. Two other tables are occupied, taking up opposite corners of the room, one by a group of Incantrix, the other by an Angelus and a Daemonium who are holding each other's hands across the table. Siduri doesn't look at me as she pours my customary shot of golden liquor, but I notice it's a much bigger shot than usual.

When she sets my glass down in front of me, she finally flicks her gaze to mine. Her voice is low and hard. "You didn't tell me you were teaming up with the Lord of Night himself."

I take a long drink. I sorely need it. When I set my glass back down, I say, "Even if I had, would you have warned me about the Factionless starting a rebellion?"

Siduri shrugs. "You made your choice a long time ago. We're friends, Zara, but there are boundaries I must keep." She pours her own drink and raises it to her lips.

"And what if I decide to be Factionless again?" I toss back the rest of the liquor, feeling the alcohol warm my chest and sparkle through my veins.

Her eyes widen for a moment before she resumes her usual unimpressed demeanor. "So, you'd give up both Kieran and the Lord of Night? Now that's a story I must hear."

I debate internally for several long moments. If I open

up to her, I'm more likely to get the intel I need on the Factionless. I don't have to tell her *everything*…

"This is just between us, Sidi." I meet her eyes and she nods. "When I was here last seeking information about the Incantrix Selena, it was so I could gain an audience with the Lord of Night."

"To spy for Kieran," Siduri says with a shrug.

I don't bother denying it. "One thing led to another, and I got a role in the Palace of Night much closer to him than I anticipated. Then I found out that Kieran has been keeping vital information from me."

I have to pause to take in a steadying breath. I haven't said those words out loud, and they burn coming out.

"Point being, I don't know if I belong anywhere anymore. And I want to know what the Factionless are up to."

Siduri contemplates me for several long moments, gaging my truthfulness, no doubt. But my words aren't a lie. Not even a little bit.

"Sometimes," she says, taking her cup and slowing spinning it on the bar, "A storm builds long before it breaks loose." She pauses, watching as the light from one of the nearby lanterns creates prisms through the glass. "We're all so tired of this war. A war which benefits no one but the heads of each house. It was bound to happen."

"Yes, but who made it happen, and how?" I press.

"He calls himself Falling Star." Siduri shrugs. "Showed up recently. No one knows exactly who he is. He wears a hood and a mask over his eyes."

I stiffen, leaning back away from Siduri and shaking my head. "Showed up? From where?"

"Well, no one really knows. The rumors are that he came from the Waste." A dark chuckle. "More likely a gutter somewhere, a street kid no one paid attention to. It's easy to be anonymous when you're fighting for survival."

Now it's my turn to scoff. "No one would come from the Waste to be here."

As the words leave my mouth, though, I wonder. What if what lies beyond is even worse than what lies within Night? Is that even possible?

"I don't buy it either, just adds to the hype around this guy." Siduri finally takes another sip of her drink. "No one knows where he lives or anything. He shows up to strategy meetings, then disappears again."

"You've sent spies after him, naturally."

"Of course." She grins. "Slipperiest bastard I've ever known. I'll give him that, at least. And, well, he's shaking things up. Things that have long been dormant. Hopes left dead and buried ages ago."

"Where was he last seen?"

"The attack."

My stomach turns to stone. "I might have killed him."

Siduri shakes her head. "Okay, I guess shortly after the attack. Enough people saw him leaving the site of the battle to know he's alive."

"Next meeting of the rebels?"

"Not announced yet. They only spread the word an hour beforehand. Scrolls pinned to the doors of the churches in a several block radius north of here, with a symbol that gives a clue to the meeting location." She smiles. "You think you can find him when no one else could?"

"It wouldn't be the first time."

Siduri's smile turns into a grin. "You're cocky as hell, Zara. Anyone ever told you that?" I hide my own smile, and she says with a laugh, "Never trust the quiet ones."

"So, that's all you can tell me? Hang out down here at world's end until scrolls appear on church doors?"

"I've already told you too much." She pours me another shot of liquor. "Same rule you established: just between us this time. Don't go telling these faction lords you have wrapped around your finger."

Something must move across my face at her words because she lets out a low whistle. "Watch yourself, Zara." Then she straightens. "Actually, never mind. You can handle things."

She lifts her glass and clinks it against mine, and we toss back the rest of our liquor.

I stay at the tavern for another hour, discussing lighter subjects and pondering this new rebel leader no one can identify. I'm about to head out into the streets beyond and wait for news of a meeting when someone saunters in from outside, waving a piece of parchment.

"Ask and you shall receive," Siduri says from across the bar with a grin.

One look at the symbol on the scroll, which shows a

star above an arched bridge, tells me exactly where the meeting of the Factionless rebels will be held.

Looks like it's time for me to unmask the new hero of Night. And more importantly, decide if he's my enemy or my friend.

CHAPTER
TWENTY-NINE

ASHER

I t's been decades since I crossed the river into Angelus territory. They'd had a different ruler then, before Ellielle murdered him. Even the angels are devils in this city.

I can feel the expanse of Night beneath me, a roiling violet presence, as well as a taut line that stretches between me and Zara. How had we existed together in the city all this time without feeling the connection before? Was it physical proximity that created this force between us? Or actual touch, that night I'd lifted her onto my horse after the battle at the river? I hadn't known then the spark that flew between us would turn into something so powerful.

And since we healed each other, my magic inside of her and hers inside me, it's grown a thousand times stronger.

She should be here. But instead, I have Carcas and a dozen of my best Daemonium, along with four Incantrix.

The warriors all ride behind the carriage, a procession of deadly force that could bring down a force three times as large. Of course, it's still a risk, coming here. Though Ellielle would have to be insane to try anything.

On this side of the river, the city looks starkly different. The Angelus have built upon the ruins of the old city, adding towers that stretch halfway to the sky. Some are made of stone, and some are made of metal in varying shades of silver and gray. The towers are pocked with windows and open archways so the wind can blow through, or even low hanging clouds. It is at once whimsical and deeply unnatural.

Ellielle's tower sits roughly in the center of this northern part of the city, far from the river and the Waste both. It's metallic, a shade just shy of pewter, with a prismatic surface that reflects the sky and clouds slightly. As the carriage pulls up, we're greeted by a half dozen angels in black brushed-silk tunics. Their faces are emotionless as they guide us up the stone steps to the arched doorway of the tower.

One of the angels breaks off from the rest of the group to lead us within, into a high-ceiling entry hall with a staircase that spirals up the back wall. We travel up, up, and further up, until the clouds slide by the windows. At last we reach another large hall, this one set with stained glass windows at the back, and a throne of black metal. Ellielle sits waiting for us, resplendent with her black hair and silver wings.

"My Lord," she says, bowing her head to me, though it

is she on the throne. "I'm so pleased you accepted my invitation."

I offer her my own slight bow, out of courtesy, not requirement. "Your offer was quite enticing. If you indeed have something that can help end this war, I would very much like to see it. I grow tired of the fighting and the suffering of Night, as do we all."

The Lady of House Angelus nods her head. She's flanked by two advisors who stand on the dais with her to the right of the throne, and another dozen angels are scattered about the room. The stained glass throws a pattern of blue and gold and green across the stone floor. We are high enough above the swirling mists of the Waste that the sun can actually reach this place.

"I trust your journey here was uneventful?" Ellielle asks, brows lifted.

I offer up a small smile. "Compared to the last time I rode in a carriage, I'd say so."

"The attack last night is all the more reason I'm glad you came. So we can put an end to this chaos." Her lips are set in a grim line, her eyes flickering with worry.

"I couldn't agree more."

"Well, can I offer you refreshments first, My Lord?" Ellielle raises a hand to gesture to her servants standing in the far corner of the room.

"Perhaps later." I clasp my hands in front of me loosely, trying to hide my agitation at being this far from my palace, and from Zara. The wild magic stirs within me, prickling through my veins and up the back up my spine. "I am eager to see this weapon of yours."

"Very well." Another gesture of her hand calls off the servants, and Ellielle stands. "We will need to cross over to the adjacent building."

As we proceed down the tower steps, which seems an arduous journey up and down for such a brief conversation, I try to settle the hope that burns in my chest. In all likelihood, whatever Ellielle thinks she possesses is not going to unify the houses and bring about an end to the war. This is Night, not a land of fairytales. I wish it could be so, but I learned long ago that such things happen in bedside tales and campfire stories only.

But *still*... I would not be here if I didn't cradle a spark of yearning deep within.

When we reach ground level again, Ellielle and her advisors lead us across a large courtyard to an old stone church. It's a large building which hasn't been added onto like some of the towers, so in comparison it's close to the earth. We enter through double wooden doors, traverse the length of the nave past rows of old pews, and then pass through another door behind the altar.

I pause at the opening, seeing a set of stairs leading down beneath the earth. Catacombs, or cellars. As if sensing my thought, Ellielle turns and looks up at me. "It seemed safest to keep the weapon beneath the earth. You'll see why in a moment."

Intrigue tickles across my skin and I follow her down. The passage turns sharply after a dozen steps.

Another dozen steps down we enter a large room filled with sarcophagi, a catacomb for royalty and church leadership, no doubt. On the far side of the room stands a strange glass box, about eight feet square. Iron bands run along the edges and frame a small doorway within.

An orb of purplish magic hovers in the air in the center of the glass box.

I cock my head to the side as the wild magic within me connects to the wild magic floating behind the glass. I've never seen it trapped in such a way, no conduit, no one to wield it.

"What exactly is this?" I ask Ellielle, my eyes meeting hers.

"This is the future," she says with a smile, striding toward the glass.

She enters the box and approaches the orb of magic, which shivers and spins as if sensing her. I walk closer, and I can see the orb actually isn't completely free floating, it extends from a thin piece of glass rising up from the floor, which ends in a smaller translucent glass ball. It seems to keep the orb in place as Ellielle makes a circle around it, her eyes flicking between me and the weapon before her.

"We've created a way to control the wild magic," she explains. "With your help, we can draw all excess magic into the box, stopping the pointless deaths and battle over it. If we possess the magic, the other factions will have no choice but to give up their arms and obey."

"But... *how*?" I ask, my mind trying to comprehend what I'm seeing. "How did you create this?"

"My best angels and witches have been working for years to figure it out. If magic is no longer part of the equation, there's nothing to fight over." Ellielle shrugs and smiles.

I meet her gaze. "You and I, we would still wield it, though."

"Of course. And perhaps our trusted advisors and warriors as well." She beckons for me to join her inside the box, then she turns and stands by the orb, her fingers hovering just inches above it. "As you can see, I've already used it to siphon magic from some of my warriors. Just to test it out, make sure it's safe."

I pause in the doorway, watching her in both fascination and trepidation. "And the siphoning didn't harm them?"

Ellielle shakes her head. "Not at all."

"They are completely unmagicked now?" A shudder runs through me. Magic is the bane of my existence, and yet the thought of not having it at all is... horrifying.

"Yes," she says. "They volunteered. As I think many other citizens would, if they knew they were no longer subject to the terrible accidents and deaths caused by surges in the wild magic, or a spell gone wrong."

Another shiver as I imagine those who die every time I lose my grip as the conduit of this wild force. "And the ones who don't want to give it up?"

Ellielle's eyes grow cold. "Sometimes people don't

know what's best for them. The alternative is centuries more of this struggle for power. A struggle that can easily be removed if the reason for the fighting is taken away."

"Show me." I nod sharply toward the orb. "I want to see the siphoning."

She nods. "Very well. I'll place a small amount of my magic into the orb. That way you can see the extent to which I trust what we've designed."

A pulse of surprise moves through me. I'd expected her to summon a servant.

Ellielle pulls her gaze from mine and reaches out to grasp the glass orb. It pulsates, and then Ellielle stiffens slightly as the magic from the orb expands. Magic begins to flow from her body into the orb. After several moments, she removes her hand and the power transfer stops.

"There." She meets my eyes again, expression triumphant. "Satisfied?"

My head is still spinning with the implications of what she's built, but I nod. "That's quite remarkable."

Curiosity gets the better of me, and I step through the door. It seems the rod acts as my amulet does, trapping magic within it, or in this case, within the walls of the box. I slowly approach the orb, and Ellielle steps to the side to allow me space. My fingers reach out, hesitating only a moment before grasping the glass orb.

I feel a surge of power and a rumble beneath my feet as Night shifts, and then blackness falls around me like a curtain.

CHAPTER

THIRTY

ZARA

T here's a very subtle trickle of people moving toward the location of Falling Star's meeting. People standing in doorways, their eyes darting down the street to see who's coming. Others strolling very casually, one at a time, stopping to inspect gardens and statues along the way as if in no hurry. I catch it all because it's what I do, and because I've wrapped shadows around me, so no one knows I am watching.

No doubt I'd be recognized at this meeting, and that won't do at all.

When I reach the old, overgrown park, I move among the trees, avoiding the path that leads to the arched stone bridge. Giant weeping willows cascade over grassy spaces littered with fallen auburn leaves. Brambles have claimed most everything else: flower beds, bird baths, stone walls. It must have been beautiful once, lush and green. Ravens flit here and there, their cries breaking the eerie silence.

I stop and stand against one of the trees about a hundred feet from the bridge. The bark is rough against my back, even through my jacket. It's still another half hour before the meeting, and only two other people traverse the park. I doubt anyone will approach the bridge until Falling Star arrives. But the park is large, with plenty of places for people to meander until the time is right.

As I wait, my mind wanders. I truly don't know what I'm going to do. It feels as if my life sits on a knife's blade, and it could slide off in any direction. Should I go back to Kieran, despite what I now know? That's what loyalty is, isn't it? Surely, I can't—and won't—choose the Lord of Night over the man who took me in all those years ago. And then there is Falling Star. What if the impossibility of my choice between Kieran and Asher *is* the answer? What if I don't have to choose either of them?

With incredible punctuality, the enigma I've been watching for arrives right on the hour, announced by the ringing of old church bells nearby. I hadn't seen him arrive, he simply *appeared*. A shiver runs over me. Can he bend shadows like I can? I'm not the only one, but with the wild magic being so unstable and that skillset requiring a lot of it, there's a reason there aren't many of us.

He is as described, cloaked and masked. The cloak is black and the mask a dusky blue, just a strip of cloth with slits for the eyes. His movements are lithe, feline. He strides to the top of the arched bridge and the Factionless come forth, melting out of bushes and paths and from behind trees like my own. There are maybe two dozen of them.

"Thank you for coming," Falling Star calls.

His voice holds a lyrical note to it, and he speaks softly so I have no choice but to move closer. I try to make out details of his nose and mouth, memorize them for later use, but it's like my eyes slide off of him. A groan escapes me. He's definitely bending shadows.

"The attack last night had unfortunate results," Falling Star says. "My heart goes out to those we lost and their families."

He bows his head for a moment of silence, and the other Factionless follow suit.

"We knew, however, that bringing down the Lord of Night could be achieved only with great sacrifice. We must move forward with the plan, so those lives were not lost in vain," he continues.

"And what is the plan? How can we defeat the Lord of Night and his new ally as well?" someone calls from the group gathered beneath the bridge.

I tense slightly. I'd figured I would come up in this meeting, but it's still unsettling to hear it. Especially since Asher has been my greatest enemy for so long. *Ally?* I want to drop my shadows and scream to them that they're wrong.

"This new associate of the Lord of Night is unexpected," Falling Star says, a growl entering his tone. "My spies had no knowledge before the battle of a warrior with the power that one possesses. A power that might even rival the Lord himself."

A stir of dismay moves over the Factionless. People cross their arms over their chests, shooting each other grim looks, and some touch their forehead in prayer to the goddess.

"I have my people trying to find out where this new warrior came from, who they are," Falling Star continues. "We'll need to separate them before the next attack, ensure they are not together to combine their magic. Between the two of them, they wield too deadly a force."

"It's hopeless," someone calls loudly.

Falling Star smiles. "Nothing is ever hopeless, nothing impossible. If you knew the things I have seen, the places I have been, you would know this. So, I ask you instead to trust me."

Another shiver of whispers moves over the crowd, but this time people are nodding, staring at Falling Star with bright eyes. They want so badly to believe. In something, *anything*.

"For now, help me find out who this new accomplice is," Falling Star says. "That is the next step. We'll gather again in the next couple of days."

My heart goes still. So, that's the great plan of the Factionless rebels. To find *me*.

I can't dwell on it further, however, because Falling Star disappears off the arched bridge without another word. Now, of course, I know why no one's been able to track him. Because he's using shadow magic. I'm not going to be able to follow him visually, either.

Falling into stillness, I stretch out with my magical senses. I close my eyes a moment, feeling the stir of Night beneath me. Violet light hums through everything, with little surges here and there. It's like a map I sense instead of see, a glowing landscape of color with brighter spots throughout.

It doesn't take long to find the magical surge coming off Falling Star, since wielding shadows uses a good bit of magic. I open my eyes and move in the direction of the glow he creates, walking swiftly, still wrapped in my own shadows. Now that I'm locked onto him I move by feel, though I can still sense the glowing map of energy behind my eyelids. It's a strange dual sensation, a tracking skill I use only rarely.

I follow him across the park, opposite the way I came in. Falling Star moves swiftly, so I have to jog to keep up. I have an advantage in that he's not expecting anyone to be able to follow him, and I doubt he's paying attention to the magical signatures nearby. If he even can, that's a skill even more rare than shadow magic.

After leaving the park, he dips down toward the border of the Waste. We're probably about a half mile east of Siduri's Tavern, in a nearly abandoned part of the city. Few live right along the edge of the Waste. The tavern is located there because it appeals to certain clientele, but most feel too nervous about the Waste or the creatures that purportedly live there to settle right at the border.

But Falling Star clearly does not share those fears. He skirts right along the edge, past empty buildings with collapsed roofs and crumbling walls. Past old churches with the doors hanging off their hinges and ivy reclaiming the stone, pulling it back toward the earth. He does not look back, confident he's alone. A smile turns my lips. I always take pride in my work, but this hunt brings more satisfaction than most. The great Falling Star, rebel leader, who no spy in the city has been able to track.

The question, however, is what I'm going to do when I catch up to him.

If I offer to join forces with him, will he even believe me? And if I do that, it means I've decided I'm no longer part of a faction. It means turning my back on Kieran forever, turning my back on his tutelage and care the last decade. An irreversible decision.

Why then, as that thought goes through my mind, is it Asher's face I see?

Returning to the Factionless is merely returning to my roots. I'm not betraying Asher. I've been working for him on false pretenses, a spy. And hopefully, I'll be the one to cut his throat when the time is right. I owe him no allegiance. *Nothing.*

With a groan, I shake my head, bringing my focus back to Falling Star. He's about fifty feet ahead of me. The time to decide is now.

It's at that moment an agonizing pain rips through my body.

The wild magic surges and bucks beneath me so

strongly it feels almost as if the earth physically rolls. Asher's face fills my head again, but this time it's different. I can *see* him, where he is at *this* moment. And through the connection that runs between us, that taut line, ever-present since I left the Palace of Night, I can feel his pain. I fall to my knees on the hard cobblestones, head in my hands as Asher's torment rolls through me.

Falling Star whips around, somehow sensing me, and takes off.

Through the waves of pain moving over my body, I watch as Falling Star races down the street. The knuckles of my right hand are bloody where I caught myself on the stones. I can still see flashes of Asher, though now his body is motionless, lying on the floor wherever he is.

Is he dead?

The thought of it causes a spike of panic, enough to cut through the pain that has me in a vice-grip. No, if he was dead then I wouldn't still feel the connection between us. I take deep breaths to focus and shove down the emotions running through me.

I should want him dead. It would solve everything, wouldn't it? The frantic buzz running through my veins is simply because *I* want to be the one to end him. I want to look him in the eyes when I do it, so he knows it's me.

And clearly that bitch Ellielle thinks she's going to rob

201

me of that. This whole grand gesture on behalf of the Angelus was obviously a trap. *Dark goddess*—if Ellielle kills him, I will *end* her. I won't do it quickly, either. She will know the meaning of pain.

The timing, however, couldn't be worse. Falling Star is drawing further away from me by the moment, and now he knows I can track him. He may not know who I am, but he'll be on the alert now. My advantage is completely blown.

I have another choice to make, except this time I'm not sure it really is one. Because Asher's agony, while it's lessened since he passed out, feels like my own wound, and I don't know how much longer I have before Ellielle carries out whatever her plan is. A sobering thought moves through me: is our connection strong enough that killing Asher would kill me, too?

With a growl of pain and fury, I shove myself up off the cobblestones, wobbling slightly. Falling Star will have to wait. I have to get to Angelus territory as quickly as possible.

I'm going to need some help, however.

I hobble down the street, calling on my shadows again, letting the wild magic wrap around me, hold me up. The pain becomes slightly more tolerable as I move and grow accustomed to it. But if Asher wakes up it's going to get a lot worse again. I let that thought drive me, allow it to push me past the pain.

The smell of the stables hits me before it comes into view. Manure and straw and the unique scent of a horse all mixed together. It's only a couple blocks away from the tavern and has been there nearly as long. I'm already being hunted by the Factionless, so adding horse thief to my list of crimes isn't going to make things any worse.

My shadows aren't even necessary, however. There's only one stable hand in sight, taking a nap on the stacks of hay bales at the end of the barn aisle. I move softly down the aisle between the stalls, glancing at the horses on each side as I pass. Most are standing, eyes closed or half-lidded as they sleep, stomping absently at flies.

I know the right horse the moment I lay eyes on her.

The chestnut mare has her head over the stall door, ears perked. She paws impatiently and weaves back and forth, clearly unhappy with her confinement. Her eyes are bright and she pauses a moment when she sees me. She's well-built, tall and broad, but not quite as thick-legged as a battle destrier. She'll be fast, and that's what I need right now. Wild magic swirls around her.

Her bridle is hanging outside the stall door. I slip it quietly off the hook and enter her stall, pushing on her massive chest to get her to back up. I don't need to drop my shadows because animals can see through them, plus they discern energy more keenly than any other sense. The mare pins her ears slightly but obeys. As I slide the bit into her mouth, she shakes her head side to side, chomping her teeth to let me know what she could do. I smile and pat her neck.

"We're going to get along just fine," I whisper.

Her ears swivel back and forth as she listens to me.

I lead her out of her stall and down the aisle. A glance back at the stable hand a good fifty feet away tells me he hasn't heard a thing. Another smile. The mare prances alongside me. I turn my gaze back toward the street.

Where it lands on the other stable hand, who is just walking around the corner into the barn.

"Oy!" he yells.

I can see the confusion on his face. He can't see me since I'm bending shadows, but he can see the mare in her bridle, clearly being led down the aisle, reins floating in the air.

Tossing the reins over her neck, I spring onto her back, calling on magic to help me in my weakened state. The mare spins and bucks twice before I can get her head up, tightening the reins to get her under control. I straighten her so she's headed toward the street again and close my legs around her. She catapults down the aisle.

With a yell, the stable hand at the exit dives out of the way. The chestnut mare races past him, her hooves clattering on the cobblestones as we hit the street and turn right. She's agile as a cat, even at this speed. Curses rise up behind us, from both stable hands now, and they run out into the street, shaking their fists as we escape.

I don't look back. I point the mare toward Angelus territory, following the line that stretches between me and Asher. She is pure speed and fury, boundless energy like a comet in the sky.

But even as fast as she is, I can only pray it's fast enough.

THIRTY-TWO

ASHER

L ight sparks at the edge of my consciousness as I awaken. It takes several moments to remember where I am, what happened. The pain helps me get there in a hurry.

I let out a growl as it lances through me. My eyes blink open and I look around. I'm not in the glass box anymore. The room I'm in now is small and circular, and judging by the tiny windows near the top, it's at the top of a tower. Wisps of cloud float by, and the wind whistles through the openings.

My arms shake as I push myself into an upright position. It feels as if all the blood has been drained from my body. My bones feel heavy, and... cold. Everything hurts, a pulsating throb that emanates from my heart. As if the very beats that keep me alive are the source of my suffering.

I force myself to my knees, and then, slowly upright. A

fresh wave of agony washes through me and I stagger into the nearby wall. My head spins and the cold stone presses into my cheek. Hunger courses through me with a savagery that takes my breath away. I've never felt hunger like this, not ever. My vision pulses red with the desire for blood.

The door to the room creaks on rusty hinges and opens. Ellielle stands there.

"My guards told me you'd finally awakened."

"What did you do to me?" I snarl.

Anger propels me off the wall and across the room, but when I reach the doorway, I smack into an invisible barrier. Magic flashes, and I stumble backwards.

"Calm down, Asher," Ellielle says with a patronizing smile. "In your state, you can't afford to expend that much energy."

"You will address me properly, as befits your ruler." I glare at her with deadly intent, calling on my magic to blast through the barrier and show her the meaning of respect.

Except it's not there.

I can't feel the wild magic at all.

My hand flies to the amulet around my neck, but even that is empty of energy. Just a piece of jewelry now, nothing more. Even the demon fire that usually burns within me is nothing but smoldering coals.

Ellielle chuckles, arms crossed over her chest. "I think it's time we renegotiate our relationship, *Asher*."

"*How?* How did you take my magic?" I pace back and

forth in front of the door. Ellielle is a foot away but completely outside my reach. It's beyond infuriating. "I watched you use the siphon, and it didn't do this to you."

A smile crosses her face. "I told you we've been working on this weapon for years. By years I mean decades. Three, to be exact. Once we had a rudimentary siphon developed, I subjected myself to it every day until I learned to control the flow." She pauses as if searching for the right words. "Think of it like... building an immunity to poison."

"You've been planning this for that long?"

"With a war that's raged on for centuries, time is all we have," Ellielle says. "I had to ensure this weapon I was building couldn't one day be used against me." She pauses again, her eyes locked onto mine. "But the real trick was adding a curse to the box that would only be triggered by your presence. That pain you feel? It's not just your lack of magic. It's a hex designed specifically for you by my Incantrix, to make sure you're too weak to get out of this. Your life rests *entirely* in my hands."

A stillness washes over me, a heaviness in my gut. "What of Carcus and my warriors?"

"They died admirably trying to rescue you." Ellielle smirks. "You would have been proud. But they were no match for my weapon, with all your magic inside it. It took only the tiniest fraction of that trapped power to end them."

Rage and shock flame through my chest. My brain begins to peel back the layers of realization of my situation. I'm imprisoned with no magic, no means of escape. Ellielle has siphoned all of my power into the glass box. A weapon which can contain wild magic...but can it truly control it?

"You have no idea the implications of what you've done," I growl. "You don't know what the wild magic really is, what Night is."

She cocks her head to the side. "You speak of it as if it's a living force."

"It *is*." I want to hit something, to punch my fist into the stone wall over and over again. "You have to let me out of here, Ellielle. Before something terrible happens."

"I think not." Her eyes narrow. "Do you think I'm an idiot, Asher? Your claim is quite convenient, and I don't trust a word out of your lying mouth."

"I'm not lying." I go still. Nothing I say is going to sway her. "You'll see, soon enough. Without a living conduit, the wild magic is going to break loose, and the results will be catastrophic."

Ellielle's gaze flickers, but her pink lips just stretch tighter across her mouth. "I guess we'll find out soon enough, then."

We stare at each other a moment in silence, and then I say, "Why not just kill me?"

She laughs. "So eager to end it all? You've given up much easier than I anticipated. How disappointing."

"Not at all," I say with a cold smile. "Just curious what your plan is for me. You've hexed me and drained me of my magic. Now what?"

Ellielle smiles in return. "I had hoped you'd entertain a proposition. Well, a proposal, more specifically."

My brow wrinkles and I shake my head. "Proposal?"

"Literally," she says. "If we marry, that ensures the Daemonium don't try to retaliate against me. And with our houses combined, the other two, along with these new Factionless rebels, won't dare challenge us."

"You must be joking." Even in my weakened state, a raucous laugh erupts from my lips. "You torture me and steal my power, and now you think I want to wed you?"

"It's not about *wanting*," Ellielle says. "It's just practicality." She shrugs. "I let you live, you tell the Daemonium all is well. None of your people have to die needlessly." Her gaze sharpens, bores into me. "I won't have to use the incredible store of wild magic to level your entire faction."

I don't care deeply for my own safety. In fact, there's a small part of me, a part buried deep within, that feels relieved I'm no longer the conduit of the wild magic, responsible for the fate of the entire city.

But my faction is another matter.

"Do not think the Daemonium die so easily, angel." My words are the rumble of thunder, the heart of a storm breaking.

But Ellielle merely smiles. "Think on it, *My Lord*." Her words twist with sarcasm. "And think quickly. My offer expires in an hour."

THIRTY-THREE
ZARA

When I approach the river, I slow the mare. I'd made it thus far without much fanfare, taking roads I know to be infrequently traveled. But now I have to get across the bridge into Angelus territory, which is guarded by Syreni on one side and Angelus on the other.

I stop in an alleyway with a clear sight of the bridge. The mare's sides heave beneath my legs, and her chest is flecked with sweat and foam from her mouth. She'd showed no signs of flagging the last few miles, but now that we're stopped she doesn't prance or paw as she had back at the stable.

The only option I see is to blast my way through with magic. I'm confident I can get across the bridge. But after that, I'll have enemies after me that are faster than this horse. Enemies that can fly.

Well, that's my only option mounted. If I leave the

horse, I can fall back on my usual tricks: shadows and stealth. I can sneak across the bridge with no one the wiser. The only problem with that option is speed, in that I'll have none.

I debate my choices for several moments, then swing off the mare, tying the reins to a sturdy pipe along the alley wall. Leaving her is going to slow my progress, but I've made it the majority of the way. Asher is being held about a mile away, and I can jog once I get past the bridge. It's a risk I'll have to take, as I'm sure to get caught by the Angelus otherwise.

I pat her on the neck, pull my shadows even tighter around me, and stride for the bridge.

Passing the Syreni guards, two Incantrix who stand on each side of the entry, is easy enough. One of them turns in my direction as if sensing my magic, but seeing no one, she shakes her head and casts her gaze outward again. I continue quietly and swiftly across the bridge.

I've crossed the island in the middle section of the bridge and am approaching the Angelus guards on the far side when Asher regains consciousness and his pain crashes into me.

I stagger, falling against the railing of the bridge on my left. The Angelus, three of them, all whip toward the sound.

Gritting my teeth, I force myself upright again. The Angelus march toward me, their brows furrowed with deadly intent, eyes scanning back and forth for the source of the sound. Another ten feet and they'll be on me.

Pushing past the fire in my limbs, I drag myself up onto the sides of the bridge, standing on the wide stone railing. As they stride toward me, I walk softly along it, grateful for my soft leather boots which are just about the most essential tool of my trade. We pass each other, but I don't quicken my pace. What's vital is getting off this bridge without being discovered. I can't afford to make more noise, raise an alarm, and have everyone out looking for me.

Within another few steps, I reach the end of the bridge and carefully jump down. A glance over my shoulder shows the Angelus guards speaking tersely with the Syreni guards in the middle of the bridge. I jog forward, not looking back again.

Every stride burns, every dozen feet I gain only by great effort. It seems impossible to keep going, but I do because I *must*. The closer I get to Asher, the stronger I feel his pain, the stronger I feel our connection. I don't have to know where I'm going because he pulls me like a magnet.

It feels like an eternity later that I reach a tall stone tower. I slip between the two guards at the door. There is no one else beyond the threshold, just a set of spiral stairs. I begin to climb, head throbbing, veins sparking as if lightning runs through them. The stairs continue up and up and up until I begin to wonder if this tower stretches to the sun.

Voices stop me as I reach the apex at last. The pain is so intense at this point that I can barely see straight. Sheer willpower is the only thing holding me together. A desire to live, and a desire for vengeance on the one who did this to Asher. The woman who attempted to rob me of justice and a decade's worth of planning.

I step slowly and softly around the last bend of the stairs until Ellielle comes into view, along with two guards. It's her voice I hear, clear and musical, yet laced with malice.

"So, you choose death, then? Not only for you, but for all Daemonium?" Power radiates off of her and her wings flare out, beating the air slowly.

"I will not live as your prisoner, Ellielle. You judged me poorly if you thought I would ever agree to that."

Asher's voice, though I can't see him from my vantage point. I take another couple of steps, ever so slowly up the stairs, until he comes into view.

"If you think you're calling my bluff, you are mistaken, Asher." Ellielle's voice is cold as a thousand winter nights, a thousand dark graves.

"I do not doubt you will carry out your plan." Asher hooks his gaze onto hers. "Do your worst. See what happens."

"Very well."

Ellielle raises both hands, magic shimmering between her palms.

There's only one choice now, so I don't take time to think on it. I open myself to the wild magic and I let it pour through me into Ellielle and the guards. A stream of raw, violet power courses through my body. My pain vanishes in the torrent of it. It hits the guards first, dropping them where they stand, then it blasts into Ellielle, flinging her against the wall. There's a shimmer and a pop around the circumference of the tower, which I realize a moment later was a magical seal keeping Asher locked inside.

A glance at all three Angelus tells me they're out cold. I rush forward, dropping my cloak of shadows. Not that he couldn't sense me coming.

"Zara," Asher gasps throatily. "Don't come any closer."

I stop mid-step. His face is twisted with torment, his jaw tight, hands fisted at his sides. "What's wrong?"

"She took my magic," he says. "And the *hunger*... I can't control it."

I see it now; his eyes are wild with it. It's not just the pain, it's raw desire, a need that burns like stars.

We don't have time for this, not if we want to get out of here. "I'll give you magic and blood both."

He hesitates still, his whole body rigid as he tries to maintain control.

The wild magic is still burning through me, a glow pulsing off my skin. "Asher, I need you to—"

I can't even finish my sentence. He growls and closes the distance between us in two long strides. One hand snakes around the small of my back, pulling me into him, and with the other he grabs a fistful of my hair, exposing my neck and tilting my head to the side in one movement. My heart ricochets like cannon fire in my chest as Asher's lips press to the delicate skin there. I tense as another rumble moves through his chest and I feel his teeth on my jugular.

I'm not prepared for the spike of ecstasy that moves through my body when his teeth enter my neck. A sound, half-moan-half-gasp, escapes my mouth. Asher pulls me even tighter against him and his cock lengthens, pressing into me. I can feel the suction of his lips against my skin as he drinks my blood, and another wave of pleasure rocks through me.

The wild magic wraps around us, its rampage coming to an abrupt halt as if this is what it wanted all along. Asher and I, joined together, sharing of each other. It moves between us, through us, until I can't tell what is mine and what is his. I can feel his strength growing again, can feel my power moving into him, filling him.

He moves his lips from my neck abruptly and claims my mouth with his tongue. I can taste my own blood, rich and metallic. Magic and life force pass between us, and I don't remember in this moment that I hate him. One of Asher's hands slides under my tunic, moving along my skin until his fingers reach my breast. His thumb swirls over my nipple and I moan into his mouth. The combination of his tongue penetrating me and his finger stroking me expertly send pleasure and power pulsating along every inch of my body.

It's the memory of the last time this happened that brings me to my senses. The last time I'd been intimate with someone, when, as the pleasure built, I'd nearly killed them. Which reminds me that I *do* want to kill Asher.

But not like this.

"Stop," I groan, shoving a hand between us. "We have to get out of here."

Asher's hand slides back down my chest, resting for a moment on my hip. I can still feel the hard length of him pressed into me and his eyes meet mine as magic sparks between us. His mouth hovers inches away. He kisses me one last time, teasing my lower lip between his teeth. A final growl moves through him, vibrating along my jaw.

Then he finally releases me.

I turn and stride from the tower room, not looking to see if he follows me. Not looking, because if I do, I don't know what I'm going to do in this moment.

I step over the bodies of the fallen Angelus. I'm not sure if they're alive or dead, and in this moment, I don't care. Emotions rage through me as I jog down the steps. Why is the wild magic drawing me and Asher together like this? It's not me, not *my* desire. I want to kill the Lord of Night, not kiss him. The wild magic, and Night with it, can go right to hell.

But yet, I can still feel the touch of his hands on my body, still feel the aftershock of the pleasure that blazed through me. I'm throbbing between my legs, and only one thing can satisfy that need. The one thing I cannot have.

I grind my teeth together and move faster.

When we hit the ground floor of the tower, I blast both of the guards out of the way with my magic. It satisfies my need to release *something*, even if it's not the thing I crave.

"I assume you can fight?" I ask Asher, looking over my shoulder before stepping out onto the street.

"I am quite revived," he says, his voice a deep purr, his eyes blazing as he looks at me.

I rip my gaze away from his and pick up a jog again. We beeline for the river, taking the same path I traveled on the way here. Most of the angels we encounter go down before they realize what's happened, stunned with a blast of magic.

The bridge looms before us within a few short minutes. Now that the pain has cleared, I can move twice as fast. One of the Angelus guards catches sight of us coming and yells. I break into a run, charging straight at them, all attempts at subterfuge abandoned. We fight our way across, which is easy with Asher and I both at full power.

And then we are back in Daemonium territory.

I lead the way back to the place I'd tied the horse. I'm less worried about our journey back to the Palace of Night, I could go on foot. But I don't want to leave her there with no food and water. She'd taken care of me, and I intend to return the favor. She nickers as I approach, giving me a look that clearly illustrates her feelings about being left.

The chestnut mare prances as I lead her out of the alleyway. I hop astride her first, then offer Asher my arm so he can follow. He slides into places behind me, and my mind goes back to that first night, after he found me on the bridge. So little time has passed, and yet *everything* has changed.

This time I ride in the lead, Asher behind me. It's his

arm around me, not mine around him. He cradles the spot just below my ribcage in an almost protective gesture. Protective… or as if I am *his*. He is warm and solid behind me, his breath in my hair.

We travel the first quarter mile in silence, and then he says, softly, "She killed them all."

I tense against him, waiting for him to continue.

"Carcas, and a dozen of my best warriors. Daemonium and Incantrix I have known for centuries." His arm tightens around me, and a shimmer of demon heat moves over him. "Ellielle is going to pay for this. I will *destroy* her."

"I'm sorry," I respond softly. And I realize, as the words leave my mouth, that I actually am. Through our connection, I can't help but feel the depth of his pain and sorrow.

"If they thought they knew war before," Asher says, his voice low and deadly, "They will come to realize how very wrong they were."

THIRTY-FOUR

ASHER

W hen we reach the Palace of Night, I begin calling commands before we even dismount.

"Summon the generals," I call to one of the footmen. "Have them meet me in the Chamber of Souls in a quarter hour."

Zara starts to lead the mare toward the stables, but I grab her shoulder.

"You are coming with me."

She opens her mouth as if to protest, but I take the reins of the horse and hand them to one of the other servants. "Make sure this horse is well tended to," I instruct the woman who takes the mare.

I stride across the courtyard and Zara follows. We reach the chamber in less than five minutes. Zara's gaze travels around the room, taking in the silver plaques on the wall. I begin pacing back and forth, my mind racing furiously, but her question interrupts my thoughts.

"What are these?"

My jaw rolls. "The fallen."

Her eyes widen as they move down the length of the wall, taking in how very many names there are. "Casualties of war?" she whispers.

I nod. Since I'd regained my strength and we'd made it across the river, my rage has grown with each minute that passes. It feels like all the anger of the world lives inside me, a fury as big as the night sky and all the burning stars within.

Zara watches me, I can feel the weight of her gaze. After several moments she speaks, softly, as if afraid I'll explode.

"How did she steal your magic?"

I haven't told her what happened yet. We'd ridden back to the palace mostly in silence, each in our own thoughts.

No one knows yet the horrific things that I know.

"Ellielle has built a great and terrible weapon." My eyes flick to Zara's as I stride back and forth. "It's a siphon and a prison for magic. It took my power and trapped it inside."

Zara blinks a couple times, then she says, very slowly, "Are you saying Ellielle still has your magic? *All* that you previously possessed?"

"It's hard to tell where my magic ends and Night begins. But yes. Suffice it to say she took all of mine and more, as the wild magic continued to flow through me."

"She could demolish the entire city with that much power," Zara says, her voice rising several octaves.

"What she intends is to take everyone's magic but a select few. Once she has all of that magic? I have no idea what her plan is." A snort escapes my lips. "She thought to marry me so the Daemonium wouldn't strike back at her for abducting me and murdering the others."

Zara's lips part in shock. "Ellielle wants to *marry* you?"

"She did." I smile, bitter and unkind. "Now that you blasted her unconscious and we escaped, I doubt the offer is still on the table."

Anger and several other emotions pass rapid-fire over Zara's face. She falls silent for several long moments. "What are we going to do?" she finally asks.

I pause in my pacing, looking at her where she's sitting against the edge of the table. Something in her tone, both vulnerable and determined at the same time, draws me closer to her. That, and her use of the word *we*.

My feet lead me to where she rests, stopping just shy of my thighs brushing against hers. "I don't know yet."

Zara's eyes meet mine. I can smell her skin, her magic, her blood. Never in my life have I tasted anything like her blood. I don't know if it was her magic or some other wondrous quality, but it'd been like drinking starlight. Something pure and sweet and holy. And the way Zara herself reacted—as if me drinking from her brought her pleasure... that was far from ordinary.

I'd been so distracted getting out of Angelus territory and back here so I could save my faction that I hadn't stopped to think about what transpired in that tower. But with Zara so close to me, it all comes flooding back. The feel of her body against mine, the sounds she made…

I've never believed in a fate other than the one I brought upon myself over two centuries ago. A fate both dark and terrible. Looking at Zara now, I realize with sudden and stunning clarity that not all things fated are evil.

Because she *is* my fate. She is mine and I am hers. She saved me, and together we will save this city. I've never been more sure of anything in my life.

A rumble moves through me, and the fire of my demon spikes from chest to groin. I lean in toward Zara, placing one hand on either side of her on the table. Her legs part slightly as I shift between them, my hard cock bumping up against her. A small sound escapes her lips, and I slowly move the cascade of her raven hair to one side, revealing the pristine column of her throat. My lips graze the soft skin just below her ear, moving down, feeling her pulse against my mouth…

Footsteps ring out in the hall, and someone clears their throat at the door.

I straighten as Malara enters the room, eyebrows arched. Zara blushes and steps to the side out of the cage of my arms. Helios walks in a moment later.

"Where is Carcas?" Helios asks in his deadpan manner as he takes a seat.

"Dead," I respond, striding to the head of the table to take my own.

Silence falls. Helios is expressionless, and Malara looks murderous.

"What happened?" she demands.

I take a moment to gather my thoughts and gesture for Zara to sit beside me, as she still hasn't taken a seat. Both of my generals' eyes follow her as she sits at my left side near the end of the table.

I tell them everything. The weapon, the ambush, Zara's rescue. When I am done, I am met with more stunned silence.

"Ellielle is no doubt planning to attack imminently, either with magic or force or both," I say.

"Agreed." Helios looks as unperturbed as usual. "We should have the Incantrix build a forcefield spell right away."

"And send the Daemonium to deal with Ellielle and her treasonous angels," Malara adds with a growl.

"A forcefield won't withstand that much wild magic," Zara says. "We need to evacuate immediately. Come up with a plan after we regroup from a safe location."

Malara and Helios both look at Zara as if she's some sort of creature who crawled up out of the gutter.

"Evacuate the Palace of Night?" Malara asks scornfully.

Helios adds, "What place do you consider a safer location than this palace?"

"*Any* place is safer right now." Zara's eyes are hard as she looks at the two of them, and then she flicks her gaze to me. "Ellielle could attack from safe in her tower, any moment now, because she knows exactly where we are."

I lean back in my chair, appraising the three of them. "It's possible the only reason she hasn't yet attacked is because she's waiting for me to make my way back, in hopes that a second attempt at murder will succeed."

"You can't possibly be considering abandoning your home," Malara snarls, narrowing her eyes and glaring at Zara.

"Zara's words are wise." I level the full force of my gaze at Malara. "Unless you're questioning who I choose to bring to my table?"

Malara's words are acid coming off her tongue. "Of course not, My Lord."

"We will implement all three ideas," I say. "Evacuation first, shielding by the Incantrix, then an offensive attack with Daemonium forces."

Helios pins his gaze on Zara. "Where, might I ask, do you suggest we evacuate to?"

"There's an old castle not far to the south," Zara answers, without hesitation. "Castle Umbra. It's abandoned, nothing like the facilities you have here, but it will do."

Helios and Malara turn their gazes to me for final approval, and I nod. "I want the palace evacuated within twenty minutes. Take nothing but weapons. The rest can be determined later."

I stand and the others follow suit. "Zara, I want you waiting by the palace gates to lead the way. Malara, you

summon the Incantrix. Helios, you will lead both Carcas'
Daemonium and your own."

The next quarter hour passes in a flurry. Horns of battle
are blown and the residents of the palace all swarm into
the courtyard, where my generals organize them into
battalions. At my signal, Zara leads the march to our safe-
house astride her fiery mare. I watch her until she disappears, waiting until the last of my faction has passed
through the gates.

I cast one last look at the now empty Palace of Night,
my family home for centuries. I would never have imagined the day would come when I would abandon it. It has
been my cage and my place of refuge both.

My fingers graze the metal bars of the palace gates as I
walk away. I don't look back again.

THIRTY-FIVE
ZARA

I can feel the eyes of both Daemonium and Incantrix on my back and hear their whispers as we travel. Asher has once again put me in the spotlight in a most unpleasant way. Both now, leading his warriors through Night to an undisclosed location, and back in the Chamber of Souls with his generals.

When we reach the abandoned castle, it doesn't get any better. The castle is dilapidated, the eastern wall partially crumbled. Safe, except for that wing, but bare of most furniture and smaller than the Palace of Night. Ivy covers the outside, and cobwebs criss-cross the interior corridors. The occasional rat scurries here and there.

And most significantly, there is no great explosion of magic from the direction we'd come. An hour passes, and then two, and the city is eerily quiet.

So, not only is everyone still unhappy that Asher has

shown such trust in me, but now I've led them all away from their comfortable home to a much lesser one because of an attack that hasn't happened.

I spend several hours trying to assist with getting a base camp set up in the castle, but everywhere I turn I catch voices gossiping about the new Incantrix and how she has the Lord of Night wrapped around her finger. And many more things of a far less pleasant nature.

I need to leave this place. Find Falling Star again and find out how I can help the rebellion. I'd made up my mind earlier. What am I even doing here?

Saving Asher from the Angelus hadn't been a choice. His pain was causing my own pain. Now that I've made sure he's safe, it's time to get out of here, especially after what happened in the Chamber of Souls. I'd told myself after our intimate experience in Ellielle's tower that I wouldn't get close to him again. But when Asher approached me at the table, the wild magic took over and all I'd wanted was for him to sink his teeth into my flesh. To lose myself in the pleasure.

It's clear I can't trust myself anymore.

Which is why I need to slip away when everyone is in turmoil.

I lean against a wall on the second floor of the castle and take a deep breath, centering myself. My fists clench and unclench. I can do this. Pressing off the wall, I let my feet carry me down the closest set of stairs to ground level. Small campfires are burning in some of the lower rooms and all across the courtyard outside. Night has fallen without me even noticing. It's grown quite cold, the air holding a kiss of the winter to come.

Before stepping out into the courtyard I summon my magic, calling the shadows. The first tingle of power is rushing through my fingertips when I hear a voice call my name.

Malara.

"There you are," the general of the Incantrix says. Her long hair is pinned into a knot at the top of her head, and her cheeks are pink from the cold. She stares at me with her purple eyes.

"Is there a meeting?" I ask.

"Soon," she says. "But that's not why I'm here."

We lock gazes and I stay silent, waiting for her to continue. She moves toward a dark corridor lit by flickering torchlight several dozen feet away, nodding her head for me to follow. Once we're away from any listening ears, she stops and begins to speak.

"I want to know more about you," she says. Her arms are crossed over her leather-clad chest. "Our Lord has taken such an interest in you, but I don't think anyone really knows where you came from or why you chose to join the Daemonium after being Factionless your whole life."

I shrug. "My parents died when I was young. I got in with a bad crowd. Went to the prison camp for a few years. Escaped. I've been on my own ever since."

It's mostly true. Even within the Animus faction, I was on my own for the most part. I've always been the only one like me. Alone with my secret, a secret only Night knew... until these last few days.

"But why the Palace of Night? Why now?" Malara's eyes bore into me. "Many think that you're a spy..." It's a threat, with only the thinnest of gossamer veils over it.

I manage to keep my posture relaxed. I'd gone over such scenarios in my head, naturally. "I can't really control what rumors spread. People think what they want to think. Say what they want to say."

She cocks her head to the side, a tight smile turning her lips. "It's easy to feel that way when the Lord of Night is so enamored with you. Were that to change, you would not be so flippant."

"I have been disliked by most my entire life," I say. "It's not flippancy, it's merely practice."

"And what is it you expect to find here that's different than before? What is it you want?"

I watch her face a moment in the flickering torchlight. "I want an end to this war, just like everyone else."

A muscle in Malara's cheek twitches. "And you think you can help the Lord of Night to that end?"

"I will do whatever I can to see it so."

Wind whistles through the castle, biting under the collar of my jacket. The flames shiver as we stare at each other, and our magic roils like two dogs facing off, hackles raised.

After several moments, Malara says, "And I will be watching and hoping that what you say is true."

It's my turn to smile. "If you're done threatening me, I have work to do."

I don't wait for a reply, I just turn and stride away from her, opposite the way we'd come. Given Malara's suspicions, I'll need to wait a while before attempting to escape. Even with my shadow magic, I don't need to get cocky. She is general of the Incantrix, after all, and she may have some sort of spell in place to track me.

A low growl escapes my chest. I really don't need this right now, on top of everything else. Anger burns through me and I stalk through the castle, not really paying attention to where I'm going until I find myself on one of the balconies on the third floor. The harvest crescent moon hangs heavy overhead, tinged with a persimmon tone, and the stars look like tiny chips of ice. Silver clouds move swiftly across the sky.

I walk to the crenelated wall running the perimeter of the balcony and lean over, eyes searching the city. Not for anything in particular, just watching. Making note of the landmarks I'm familiar with, memorizing details not so well known. That's how I knew about this place, merely observation during one of my many journeys through Night. My mind spins with the map of this place I call home, this place I both hate and love so very much. I don't know why there is any love at all—it's not as if my life has been happy or peaceful. The wild magic has been both a powerful tool and the cause of my loneliness.

Regardless of my complicated feelings, this city is my home. The idea of Ellielle demolishing awakens a fierceness inside of me, a creature of fury and flame.

I will defend Night.

Even to my last breath.

THIRTY-SIX

ZARA

H unger eventually summons me down from the balcony. The cool air and the stars have swept my mind of its spinning thoughts and my anger at Malara's confrontation, so I'm finally able to think straight again.

I'll leave tonight, when everyone is asleep. Take my leave of Asher and Kieran both, find Falling Star and help the Factionless best I can. It's the only option that makes me feel less... *trapped.* I'm tired of allying myself to liars and murderers. I need some time away from it all, to figure out my next steps.

I've never failed at anything in my life, but getting my revenge on the Lord of Night is going to have to wait. I'm not sure I can kill him without causing my own death. It's all come full circle again—the wild magic just doesn't seem to want him dead.

And I don't know how to live my life without this purpose, this burning vengeance.

The smell of cooking meat greets me as I step out into the courtyard of the abandoned castle. I'm grateful the kitchen staff had the foresight to carry supplies with them when they fled the Palace of Night. Not that we couldn't have foraged for food elsewhere, but it would have been a distraction we don't need right now on the brink of battle. A battle unlike any fought before.

I approach one of the makeshift cooking fires and collect a small roll and a piece of meat. The flames feel luxuriously warm against the cold night air, so I stand in the flickering light while I eat, devouring my food in a few quick bites. I've just finished when I hear my name called behind me.

"Most of us don't enjoy eating around a campfire like Factionless filth. But that's what you're used to, isn't it, Zara?"

The voice is recognizable even before I turn slowly to face her. Tryn.

She's standing there with the same group of followers who threatened me in the kitchen at the Palace of Night. They stand in the shadows, just beyond the circle of fire-light. Several of them already have magic palmed in their hands, glowing or sparking against the courtyard stones.

"I've never lived in a palace before, it's true." I shrug. "Didn't realize that was an indicator of one's worth."

"Why did you bring us here anyway, traitor?" calls one of the Daemonium standing next to Tryn. "How exactly is living on the streets going to help us in the battle ahead?"

"I heard you were scared the Angelus would blow up the palace," another snarls. "Now we're sleeping on ice-cold stone in a rat-infested castle because of you."

"Apologies for trying to keep everyone safe." I cross my arms over my chest as a flare of heat moves through my chest. "Now, if you'll excuse me, I'll go find some of those rats, being as how they're better company than what's in front of me."

When the ball of magic flies at my face, I duck and wrap shadows around me. A smile curls my lips—a fight is exactly what I need right now to let out all my pent-up emotions.

I spring from my crouch, releasing a blast of magic that sends them onto their backs. Tryn screams a curse and hurls another ball of magic toward me, which I easily avoid. The wild magic surges into me, crackling like lightning between my hands as I wait to allow them time to crawl to their feet. A lady always helps her opponents up. So she can knock them on their asses again.

A crowd has gathered around us now, dozens of Daemonium and Incantrix forming a circle around me and Tryn's entourage. I hear more curses and taunts called, all of them aimed at me. It seems I only have one friend in this faction, which is fine by me. And Elyse is nowhere in sight.

When six blasts of magic fly toward me, I have to be a bit quicker on my feet, spinning my shadows, diving and ducking and throwing my own counterattack. I'm feeling quite pleased with myself for having the upper hand in a fight six-against-one when the bolt of magic hits me square in the back.

I fall to my knees on the courtyard stones which sends an extra wave of pain through my limbs, on top of the electric agony that races up my spine where I'd been hit by some coward from behind. A chorus of cheers rings across the crowd. I jump to my feet, spinning to face the low-life who attacked me from behind, when suddenly a surge of power washes across the entire courtyard.

Power I'd recognize anywhere.

Asher strides through the masses of his warriors, a god of death and vengeance, palpable rage pouring off of him. The crowd scatters like the rats they mocked, everyone's faces turning from sadistic glee to terror in an instant.

He moves toward me as if I'm the one he's angry with. When he reaches me, he circles like a wolf, eyes locked on mine, magic merging, hips brushing. My heart races in my chest, trying to escape through my throat.

In one swift movement, he grabs me and throws me over one of his shoulders, knocking the wind out of me in a *whoosh.*

His voice booms out across the courtyard, thunder and flame both.

"Zara is *mine*. She is not to be harmed. She is not to be spoken ill of. Any insult or injury to her is insult and injury to *me*."

He turns in a circle, raking his gaze across the crowd.

"Any who disobey or so much as question my judgement in this matter will suffer at my hand. Am I understood?"

His words echo and magic crackles across the courtyard. Everyone around us drops to one knee in fealty, their heads bowed.

Asher doesn't linger further. He stalks back across the courtyard. The blood is rushing to my head where I bounce upside down, still slung over his body. My initial shock is wearing off, and in its place comes fury. I can't see well from my vantage point, but I feel it when he begins to climb a set of stairs. I pound my fists into him, but he ignores me. He ascends to the third floor, heads down a hallway into a large room, and then deposits me unceremoniously on a huge four poster bed.

"How dare you!" I hiss, scrambling up onto my elbows.

The room spins as my head tries to regain equilibrium. A cold wind rushes in from a set of windows behind the bed, which helps clear the spinning sensation.

Asher's eyebrows shoot up. "I am the *Lord of Night*. What I dare or do not dare is *entirely* my right."

"I am not *yours*." My eyes shoot arrows into him. "I am not some piece of property, or your concubine to throw around as you wish."

His voice is a deadly growl when he speaks. "You *are* mine, Zara. Whether you want to be or not."

"I don't," I snarl. "I never asked for this."

Our eyes meet and he closes the distance between us,

stepping to the edge of the bed and towering over me. Power rolls off of him and the look in his eyes is downright carnivorous. My heart spikes in my chest and my magic, very much against my bidding, flares and rolls around him as if pulling him closer. He reaches down, grabs my hand, and pulls me upright into the circle of his arms.

"You are mine, as I am *yours*," he says, a deep rumble moving through his chest.

Conflict burns in my core like a thousand fires. My anger is fading rapidly, replaced by a longing, a *craving*, that I can't control. My brain sends my hand up between us, pushing against him. I can feel his hard chest against my fingers, and his heart beating against my palm. But at the same time, my magic merges with his, drawing us together.

"It's just the wild magic," I murmur. I close my eyes and shake my head. I can't even look at him. My arm trembles I want to move it so badly, let him crash against me. Dark goddess, I *hate* this…

He reaches out and runs a finger down my cheek, sending a shiver up my spine.

"I don't think either of us thought this would happen when we first met." Asher slides his hand around the small of my back. "But fate seems to have other plans."

I shake my head back and forth. "I don't believe in fate."

"Just because you don't believe in something doesn't make it less true." Asher leans into me, pressing his face into my hair. "I can hear your heart racing, Zara. Feel your magic. I know you want this, same as me."

My heart flips as he kisses my neck. "I don't," I say shakily.

"You're a liar." Another rumble moves through his chest.

The finger that started on my cheek moves down my neck and along my collarbone. Magic sparks between us, and I'm shaking with the effort to not give in. My blood is pounding in my veins, and Asher inhales deeply, like he's taking in my scent. I don't know what I've done to deserve this dark and twisted fate...

"Do you know what I realized?" His voice is dark as his finger traces down the length of my arm. When he reaches my wrist, he circles his finger over the pulse there.

I don't answer, because I can't speak. All of my concentration is consumed by not moving toward him.

Asher lifts my hand and presses his lips to the spot his finger circled a moment before. "Since I drank your blood, your magic, my hunger has disappeared almost entirely."

A small murmur escapes my lips.

"Do you know how remarkable that is?" He says in a husky whisper. "My hunger has been an ever-present howling beast for over two centuries. Even after I feed, it's better, but still ravenous. But you...your blood..."

His teeth slide into me, puncturing my skin right at the base of my wrist. Ecstasy rolls through me and I moan, sinking against him. My other hand, the one pressed against his chest, curls and fists his tunic. Asher's hand at my waist pulls me tighter against him as he drinks.

He doesn't take much. He has control, unlike so many of the blood-drinkers, who will drain a person dry. When he pulls back from my wrist less than a minute later, a heady buzz moves through my body, as if I'm the one who just fed. Asher kisses the side of my neck.

"You are the most incredible creature I've ever met, Zara," he murmurs against my skin.

As he guides my wrist back down to my side, his fingers wander again, moving between my legs. Through my pants, he strokes against my core and I gasp as pleasure of an entirely different sort races through my body. I hate him in every way, and yet my magic and my body can't seem to stop warring against me.

"I don't want this!" I gasp.

Asher pulls back. "Want what?" he asks breathily.

I force my words out through clenched teeth as I desperately try to maintain control of myself. "I came here to work for you, not for...*this*."

Asher is silent for several long moments, his rich, metallic eyes burning into mine. He loosens his grip on me. "What is it you do want then, shadow assassin?"

"I want things I can never have." My words spark like flames from a fire, anger rushing up inside of me. "I want this war to be over. I want my life to be mine. I want my sister back—"

A smile tugs at Asher's lips. "I have news of her, actually."

Everything goes from chaos to stillness in an instant. I stiffen, my chest tightening. "What?"

"Yes. Since you told me she was in the prison camp, and all of the prison camp Incantrix come to the Palace of Night, I had someone search our records. Her transport was intercepted by Factionless and never arrived." He shakes his head. "It's not much, but it's a start. A lead. After the battle, we can look for her."

My world goes black for a moment. The cold of the night air presses against me like ice, like death, as if I'm floating among the endless stars.

When I can finally speak, my voice is hoarse and halting. "My sister is dead. She died at the Palace of Night."

Asher's brow furrows. "I assure, you, we keep very accurate records. No one by her name—Jaylen—came to the palace."

"That's not true." My words come out low and deadly. I shift out from under Asher. "I heard from a very trustworthy source that she died in *your* palace."

Asher goes still. "So…that's why you came here. Not for me, or the war. For your sister."

There's no point denying it now. I couldn't lie if I tried. "Yes."

"Well then, I'm glad I could give you some hope," he says softly, not with the anger I'd expected. "I can't be sure she hasn't since died, but it wasn't in my palace."

Just when I thought things couldn't get more complicated, this… *this…*

Tremors wrack my body. Everything I thought I

knew... The life I've lived, the truths I've held close, it all shatters within me. Destroyed, utterly and completely.

I need answers. And I can't stand here one moment longer.

I spin, wrapping shadows around me, and I jump through one of the windows behind the bed. Night whooshes around me and when I land on the street below, I hear Asher's voice boom out in the darkness, calling after me.

I don't look back. I turn, and I run.

CHAPTER

THIRTY-SEVEN

ZARA

I run for so long and so hard that when I finally stop, collapsing against the wall of an alleyway, the cold air I'm sucking into my lungs feels like blades. But the pain is good. The pain grounds me, keeps me from losing control.

Because the one thing upon which I've based my entire life's purpose is now in question.

And I'm an inch away from opening myself to the wild magic, all the way, and letting it claim me forever.

It can't be true. It *can't*. Asher must be lying, or misinformed. Kieran told me Jaylen died in the Palace of Night. That he'd confirmed it via his own spies. Why would he tell me that when I was just a teen?

I have to know the truth. And I have to know *right now*. Tonight.

It takes me an hour to travel into Animus territory. Once I sneak into Kieran's tower, it's another two hours of waiting in the dark before I finally hear footsteps on the stairs. The door opens and closes with a creak. The footsteps stop.

"Zara," he breathes.

Because of course his inner animal smells me.

He strides across the room toward me, his magic roiling within him. I summon a ball of magic in my palm and hold it up at chin level, and Kieran stops a foot away when he sees the look on my face.

"What's happened?"

A tremor runs through my body. I grind the words out between clenched teeth. "Tell me who witnessed my sister's murder."

Surprise pulses over his face. "What?"

"You heard me," I growl.

"What is this about?" He shakes his head back and forth. "I've been so worried about you…and you show up now asking about your sister?"

"Answer. The. Question." A glow emanates from my skin. My magic is so close to rupturing out of me.

Kieran runs a hand through his hair, brow furrowed. "It was one of my spies, I don't remember which one. That was ages ago."

"That's incredibly non-specific for something I've based my *every* action in life on." My words taste like acid on my tongue. Violet sparks shoot off the ball of magic in my hand.

"You need to calm down, Zara. You're too powerful to be this agitated…"

Kieran raises a hand in a placating gesture, as if I'm some wild animal.

"Don't patronize me, Kieran!" I shriek. "Are you certain my sister was murdered by the Lord of Night or not? Answer me and answer me right *now*."

It's the look on his face that confirms it. His eyes stricken, his mouth opening and closing, trying to think of what to say without me blasting him and this whole forsaken tower down around us.

"Goddess," I whisper, staggering backwards away from him. "He was right."

"Who was right? The Lord of Night?" Kieran's eyes widen. "You trust his word over mine?"

"Lord of Night?" Fury pulses through me, turning my words into the lash of a whip. "Don't you mean your brother?"

Shock registers over Kieran's face, and then he goes still. When he speaks again, his tone has changed. It holds a detachment, a chill, I've never heard in it before. "You've grown awfully close to the enemy, Zara, if he has told you such a thing."

"Don't turn this on me. You've lied to me ever since we met." I draw in a shuddering breath, my emotions shifting between rage and heartbreak each moment. "You should have told me before you sent me to the Palace of Night that Asher is your brother. You *used* me, told me my sister had been murdered, all so I'd be your perfect weapon. Your tool for vengeance."

"A leader does what he must." Kieran's eyes burn into

mine, his dragon swirling just beneath the surface. "You would understand if you were in my position."

Tears prick my eyes and I squeeze them away angrily. "I've never been anything but a pawn to you."

"I told you what I had to. You weren't going to stop looking for her unless you thought she was gone. And the truth does not make my brother any less evil. He still deserves the revenge you planned. He's done so many ruthless and terrible things… countless lives taken, an ocean of blood on his hands." Kieran shakes his head. "Even if he didn't kill your sister, he still killed Lyri. You saw that with your own eyes, you can't deny it."

"I don't." My eyes blaze into his. "He did kill her. Because *you* tried to kill him. Another plan of yours you left me out of. If you'd told me, Lyri might be alive still."

"Oh, so that is my crime now, too?" Kieran steps forward, rests his hand on my shoulder. His voice is soft and low. "What happened to you in the Palace of Night? How did he turn you against me?"

"You did that all on your own," I growl. "You're both terrible people. Both liars and murderers. And I've lived my whole life—this whole city has—caught in your deadly, endless orbit."

Kieran stiffens, his fingers flexing into my skin.

"The tragic thing is," I say, my eyes glittering with unshed tears, "You didn't have to lie about my sister. I *loved* you. I would have been your weapon anyways."

"I loved you, too, Zara." Kieran's hand slides from my

shoulder to cup my cheek. "I still do. Please believe that, if you believe nothing else."

My head swims and I close my eyes. Kieran shifts forward, his hand circling my waist. His dragon magic swirls around us. The heat of his body washes over me, too, and his lips hover over mine. I've wanted this for *so* long.

But it's all been a lie.

I open my eyes, meeting his gaze. "I don't believe anything you say anymore." I shove into his chest and step away from him.

Kieran's expression goes from stunned to furious in the span of two heartbeats. "Then he really did turn you."

I take another step away from him. "I release myself from your service, My Lord." I snarl the last two words.

"Only I can release you," Kieran growls.

"Try and stop me, then." I meet his eyes and power flashes through me, a deep violet glow. "You are *not* my equal. You never were."

"Go, then." He gestures toward the door. "Run back to your new ruler."

"I have no ruler," I say. "I belong to no one but myself now."

I leave him there, alone, in the darkness.

I will tear apart this entire city to get Zara back.

She may think she can walk out on me. I'd told her only days before that it was her choice. But that was *before*.

Before we'd healed each other after the Factionless attack.

Before she'd rescued me from Angelus territory.

Before I'd *tasted* her.

Nothing is more clear to me than that she and I exist to be together. To rule together. To tame this wild magic that controls everyone's lives. She is the counterpart to my magic, the other half of my soul. I will not let her go, not now. Not ever.

As I stand in the window and look out on the empty streets below, I can feel her drawing further and further away from me. I suck in a lungful of cold air to calm the panic that courses through my veins.

What made her so angry? She said she'd come here to find her sister, and I'd given her valuable information, promised to continue the search. But then she'd said her sister was dead, and she seemed furious I contradicted her. It all happened so fast, and then she'd been gone.

Stillness and an icy realization crawl across my skin.

Zara hadn't come to the Palace of Night to find her sister. She'd come for revenge. She'd come to *kill* me.

I begin to pace the length of the room, my cloak swirling behind me. It doesn't change things. It doesn't change the way I feel. If anything, some sadistic part of me thrills at the idea that she *could* kill me. She, and no one else.

Surely, though, once Zara realizes I didn't kill her sister, she'll return to me. I need her for the battle ahead. There's no telling how much wild magic Ellielle now has captured in that weapon of hers. Because, no doubt, that's the reason for the delay in her attack. I'd thought she was waiting until I returned to the Palace of Night, but she must want even more magic amassed before she attacks, to ensure our complete annihilation. There can be no other reason.

The scuffle of a boot brings my gaze up sharply. Helios stands in the doorway to my temporary quarters.

"My Lord," he says, bowing his head in deference. "The strategy meeting?"

"Yes. I was delayed. I can join you now."

"And will your—will the Incantrix Zara be joining us?"

I narrow my eyes, wondering if it's my imagination that emotionless Helios has the slightest edge of scorn in his tone. "She is attending to a private matter."

"Ahh."

I gesture for Helios to lead the way, and he steps back out into the hall. We travel down a long passage to the other wing of the castle, remaining on the third floor. Helios stops outside a doorway and ushers me inside a large room which seems to have been some sort of study or library. A large table sits in the center, though there are no chairs. Crumbly bookshelves line one wall. Several candles lit about the room throw shadows as I approach the table.

Malara is already standing at the table, as are all the battalion leaders, six in total, comprised of four Daemonium and two Incantrix. Aya Olora is with them as well, serving as one of my battle strategists. I nod to them as I take my place at the head.

"What news have you?" I ask, casting my gaze around.

"Nothing much, I'm afraid," Malara says. "The city is quiet. All the houses are locked up tight in their own sectors. And nothing has been heard from the Factionless rebels, either."

I clench and unclench my jaw. "That is far from normal. Something is awry."

"Agreed," Helios says, coming to stand at my left side.

"We can't sit here and wait for Ellielle to make the first move," I say. "It won't be long before someone realizes we're here. If it hasn't already happened. Then we're vulnerable once again to an attack from her weapon."

"What do you have in mind, My Lord?" Malara keeps her expression unusually neutral.

"At dawn, we will gather in the courtyard, then each battalion will travel separately toward the river." I lean over the table, gesturing with my hands. I make a wide arc to represent the river. "We'll approach in smaller groups so as to make our journey as unnoticed as possible. When we reach the river, however, we'll connect again at the bridge."

"Which battalion shall take the bridge first, My Lord?" Helios asks.

"I will lead the charge myself, with Marin's Incantrix battalion." I gesture at the woman across the table from me. "They can take down any magical barriers the Angelus may have erected, and also lay down defense for the rest of the battalions after they cross. Verok's fire battalion will come next and clear the path toward Ellielle's tower."

Marin and Verok both give me sharp nods of understanding.

"And Ellielle's weapon, My Lord—how will we destroy that?" Malara asks.

I pause for a moment. "We will have to hope that my powers, combined with Zara's, can take it down."

Silence falls, and the question of Zara's whereabouts hangs thick in the air. But no one dares ask.

"Very good, My Lord," Helios says with a stiff nod.

The others don't look quite as sure. It's the first time

I've ever been uncertain of an outcome in battle. I know it, and they know it.

This war may be over sooner than I ever imagined. Not because the residents of this city finally find peace, but because magic is stripped from everyone to feed one tyrant's delusions of control. If only Ellielle would heed my warning. The destruction it will cause if she succeeds...

I know more than anyone that Night can never be truly controlled.

I also know that I need Zara. I pray to the goddess that wherever she is, she comes to her senses and returns to me.

CHAPTER
THIRTY-NINE
ZARA

The last words I spoke to Kieran echo in my head as I stride through the night, heading south. *I belong to no one but myself now.*

But is it true?

I've lived my life beholden to both of these men. Kieran because of fealty and gratitude, and what I thought was love but now realize was just hero worship that started when I was a teen. Asher because he'd been the object of my obsession from the moment I lost my sister, the thing I fixated on to get me through the grief. My purpose, my reason for being.

All of it has been twisted now. Everything I thought I knew, erased. Rewritten.

I should feel relieved to finally be free of it, but I'm more adrift than ever before.

And I can still feel my connection to Asher, that tether

of energy that holds us together. Why does it exist? Why do the two of us possess the ability to wield the wild magic like no one else in Night?

A horrifying thought washes over me: had the magic of Night somehow sensed my fixation on Asher? Is my hatred and desire for vengeance the cause of this whole thing?

I wander the streets in a daze for an hour, then two. It must be halfway to dawn at this point. The stars spin overhead, and the air is so cold my breath comes out in little white puffs that remind me unpleasantly of angels. In the distance I hear commotion and realize I've headed straight for the tavern on instinct, without purposeful thought. But I don't want to see anyone in the state I'm in. And I certainly don't need any of Siduri's sass.

Turning from my path, I cut across a large graveyard edged with fir trees on one side, a small forest almost. Even though I have shadows wrapped around me, an owl senses my presence and hoots a warning to its friends. I weave slowly through the engraved headstones and mausoleums and statues. I feel drunk, even though I avoided the tavern.

I belong to no one…

I belong to no one…

No matter how many times I say it in my head, it doesn't lessen my sense of Asher. He's like a burning coal at the back of my chest, glowing softly, unable to be dislodged.

I let out a scream of anguish and throw a ball of magic

at one of the statues, decapitating it with a single blast. The sudden violence shocks me into silence, and then I feel tiny pricks of pain from tears welling in my eyes. I sink down with my back to one of the graves and put my head in my hands.

I hear the footsteps only a moment before the voice speaks.

"Remind me never to get on your bad side," Falling Star says, dropping the shadows cloaking him from a half dozen paces off. He raises his hands in a gesture of peace.

"What do you want?" I growl, another ball of magic in my palm in an instant. Clearly, I'd dropped my own shadows when I lost my temper.

He cocks his head to the side, his dark cloak shifting around his face. "Did you really think I wasn't going to find you after that little stunt you pulled yesterday? That's a game two can play." A chuckle slides across the night between us.

I appraise him a moment in silence. He's still using shadows to make his face blurry. He doesn't seem to want to hurt me, but I keep my magic at the ready anyway.

"Fair enough," I say with a shrug.

"Why were you following me?" he asks.

"I wanted to find out more about the little rebellion you've been planning. How you got the Factionless to come together. And... a bit just because I could, and I wanted to succeed where no one else had." I smile and offer another shrug.

"Your honesty is refreshing." I get the sense that he's

smiling, too, even though I can't see his face in detail. "But my rebellion isn't so small anymore."

I get to my feet, crossing my arms over my chest. "Could you use one more?"

Falling Star snorts. "How do I know you're not a spy?"

"Oh, I'm definitely a spy." A smirk twists my lips. "But I'm recently unemployed, and I have no loyalties or obligations to keep."

We lock gazes for several long moments.

"I suppose I can't keep you from attending the secret meetings." Falling Star taps a finger on his chin, clearly considering my offer. "We'll see where things go from there."

"Okay, then."

I feel a bit deflated at the lackluster response, but did I really think the mysterious leader of the Factionless rebels was going to welcome me with open arms at our first meeting? He's clearly a lone wolf.

Falling Star turns to go, but after a couple steps, he turns around. "Oh, and Zara? You may want to make sure you're not anywhere more than a mile north of here come tomorrow."

My eyes flare. "Why? And how do you know my name?"

His smile can be heard in his voice this time. "Let's just say the angels have some tricks up their sleeves, and I wouldn't want to be one of the Daemonium come dawn."

My heart squeezes painfully, but I just throw him a

sharp nod. "Thanks for the tip. But you still didn't say how you know..."

Falling Star vanishes before I can finish the sentence.

I pace back and forth in the graveyard. The angels have tricks up their sleeves... what does that even mean? Does Falling Star just mean Ellielle's weapon?

I should take Falling Star's advice, of course. Stay down here near the border of the Waste, avoid whatever bloodshed happens between the factions. Because I'm not a part of them anymore, I belong to no one. I don't owe anyone anything.

So why does it feel like my connection to Asher chafes even harder with this knowledge?

I still don't know if this link between us means that if he dies, I die along with him. Or if the wild magic will annihilate huge swaths of the city like it did two hundred years ago when he first became its conduit. That's the part Ellielle doesn't realize. She's playing with forces she doesn't understand, and doing so risks unleashing a far deadlier problem.

I walk back and forth for so long I'm surprised I don't wear a track in the grass beneath me. I'm trying to start a new life, strike out on my own, but I can't do that with this connection to Asher looming over me. It's not just the ever-present burn of it, it's the risk of what will happen to me if something happens to him.

Falling Star's warning rings in my ears. Asher and the rest of the Daemonium are walking into some sort of a trap, that much is clear. Asher's life, and possibly my own, are now in Ellielle's hands.

I realize that no matter what happens, I can never be free of this while Asher is alive.

And I am *done* being ruled, possessed, owned by another. If I'm going to die, it's going to be on my terms. I will *not* let fate rule me.

I turn my gaze north. There are still a couple hours until dawn. I still have time to do what I set out to do in the first place.

Night thrums within and around me as I travel toward Castle Umbra. The sky is a hue of deepest purple in the last stretch of darkness before the sun rises. Thin clouds race across the moon. My breath burns in my lungs as I run.

In what seems the blink of an eye, I am climbing the steps to the third floor of the castle. All is quiet, still. The fires in the courtyard are embers now, and only a handful of guards at the perimeter are awake. A pallor of doom hangs in the air, the residue from too many grim night-mares on the eve of battle.

I step into the doorway of Asher's room. In the dark-ness, I can see the shape of him on the bed, see the slow rise and fall of his chest as he sleeps. My fingers find the dagger in my boot, the metal hilt a cool kiss against my skin.

Silently, I move across the room until I'm standing at the foot of the bed. He's lying on his back, dark hair across his pillow, silver mask lying on the bedside table. One step, two steps take me around to the side of the bed. Another step and I'm as close as I can be.

I take a deep breath, ignoring the shiver that runs through my body.

Then I swing myself up onto the bed, straddling him and pressing the blade to his throat in a single movement.

Asher's eyes fly open. I press the knife harder until a thin line of crimson runs down his skin.

"You're here to kill me," he says calmly, though his words come out rough because of the pressure I have on his neck.

"Yes," I hiss.

We stare at each other, and my heart beats itself sense-less inside my chest.

A rumble of heat and magic moves through Asher's core. "Then why haven't you done it yet?"

I lean on the knife, spilling more of his blood. "Shut *up*." I shake my head as a fuzzy panic moves through me. "You have taken *so* much from me. I can't live my life with this connection running between us. I won't leave my fate tied to yours."

He chokes out his words. "I thought you didn't believe in fate."

"I believe I am finally taking control for the first time," I grind out between clenched teeth.

"Even if claiming my life claims your own?"

A sharp nod. "Even so."

He spreads his arms out to either side of him, a gesture of surrender. "I give you my life, then. Take it, Zara. I belong to you already." His eyes lock onto mine, spinning with sparks of magic. "Body, magic, soul. And my heart."

I let out a bark of bitter laughter. "Your heart? You *need* me. That's not the same as love. Not even close."

"I do need you. But I also want you. Covet you. Crave you." He lifts one hand and places it over my heart. "I dream of you day and night."

I can feel my heartbeat connect to the pulse in his palm. Heat and magic wash over me.

"I *hate* you," I growl, my hand shaking on the dagger.

"I know," he says.

I fling the blade away from me and crush my lips to Asher's, melting into him in a maelstrom of fury and desperation. He sits up, lifting me with him so I'm straddling his lap. Our magic crashes together with all the force and inevitability that's been building inside of me for days. I don't know why I'm fated for this darkness, these boundless desires for my greatest enemy. All I know, in this moment, is that I can't fight myself any longer.

Asher kisses me as if he's going to devour me whole, hot and hard, claiming my mouth with his tongue. The way he tangles it against mine sends shivers of wicked pleasure all the way to my core. He growls as if he can sense it, and I feel him harden between my legs. I rock my hips, grinding into him, needing to be closer, closer, closer…

"Zara," he groans against my mouth. "You are my goddess…I worship no other."

I pull off his tunic, revealing his stretch of muscles and battle scars. Mine comes off next, joining the dagger on the floor. His hands wrap around my back, and mine wind into his hair. His tongue claims my mouth again until I'm breathless and the last bit of thought and logic vanishes with the air in my lungs.

Asher makes a sound in his chest like a ravenous animal and flips me over onto my back. His teeth graze my earlobe, then his lips travel down my neck, along my collarbone, to my breasts. A gasp escapes me as he flicks his tongue over my nipple through the thin lace of my brassiere. Again, then a third time. My magic flares around us and a soft moan rises from my throat. He rips the lace where it meets between my breasts, freeing them so he can cup one as he continues to kiss down my torso.

When Asher reaches my hips, he unbuttons my pants slowly, peeling them off me along with my boots. His eyes burn into me as he kneels, kissing one hip bone, and then the other. When his lips press against my soft swirl of hair, my head swims. He plants a kiss on the inside of one thigh, then slowly runs his tongue up the length of my opening. I cry out and grab a handful of the blanket beneath me. Asher growls and buries his face between my legs.

He penetrates me with his tongue, deep and hard, arms hooked under my knees, pressing me into him. Pleasure surges through me, and another wave of magic. I can feel mine and his both, blending, spiraling together, sparking in the darkness. That part of me that's afraid to lose control, afraid my magic will be too strong, tries to hold on. But Asher's relentless assault tears me from that place I've clung to, sends me high into a stretch of endless velvet sky.

A ripple of ecstasy builds quickly, pouring outward like my magic. My back arches off the bed and my whole body begins to shake. "Asher!" I gasp. He picks up even more speed, and then I am lost to it.

A cry rips out of me, and in that moment of bliss, Asher moves his mouth to the inside of my thigh and sinks his teeth into the soft flesh there. A second explosion of pleasure moves through me and the room shakes as my magic flashes and pulses. It feels as if the world is ending and beginning all at the same time. Beneath the castle, Night rumbles.

Asher kisses his way back up my body until he finds my mouth again. Slow and soft, he kisses me until I return to myself.

I roll him over onto his back. He's wearing only silken pants, which I pull off with ease. My heart races as I reach down, fingers gliding along the enormous length of him. A groan escapes him as I explore every inch. Then, kneeling over him, I slowly slide myself onto his shaft.

We both let out cries as he enters me. I begin to rock back and forth, gyrating against him, pumping my hips while my fingernails dig into his chest. Everything about him is powerful, unbreakable. So strong. My equal, the only one I cannot hurt when I lose control.

I pick up speed as we move in rhythm together, Asher thrusting up into me as I rock down onto him. My magic is spiraling around us again, not spent yet, not even close. His mixes with it, and I don't really know if there's a difference anymore, or if we're one and the same. There is just us and this inevitable joining I've fought so hard, this connection I cannot resist.

Asher flips us again and hovers a moment before sliding back into me slowly. I gasp when he pulls back and then thrusts in again. He rolls his hips, sliding in and out of my slickness, over and over until the stars spin around us again, and the room begins to shake along with our bodies. Asher's breath comes in hard gasps, his magic pulsating off him in violet waves. When I let out a cry and convulse beneath him a second time, he thrusts once more powerfully and then yells as his own pleasure takes him.

Our magic feels like a supernova, pulsing out across the city. Beneath us, the whole of Night flares, and a loud rumble moves through the streets.

Asher collapses next to me, pulling me onto his chest and kissing my hair. Even in the cool night air we are hot and sticky, the smell of our bodies and our efforts lingering around us. I'd never thought I could have this, this total release, without hurting someone else. This changes everything… and it changes nothing.

But in this moment, I don't want to think about the future or anything else. Anything but Asher's heartbeat against my cheek, and his fingers softly stroking my back.

We stay like that for a long time, until there's a slight lightening to the color in the room, that precursor of the sun rising over us, this new day that will bring death and endings. Whether or not it also brings new beginnings is yet to be seen. The gravity of it spins slowly through the room with the afterglow of our magic.

I wish, with all the magic I possess, that I could stop time in this moment.

But I cannot.

Asher pivots slightly so we're facing each other. He gently brushes a piece of hair off my face. "I know you still feel the way you feel," he says, his voice a low rumble in his chest. "But know that I still feel the way I feel, and I meant all the things I said before. I am *yours*, Zara. Everything else may change today, but that will not."

He kisses me once, softly.

"I will not ask you to fight with us if you don't want to," he says. "This may be our last day, so that choice must be yours."

His fingers slide from my cheek to my shoulder, tracing the edge of it.

"I will fight by your side," I say. "Because it's going to take both of us to defeat Ellielle and her weapon. If we even can. After that…" I trail off, heart pounding, because I don't know where to go from here.

"After that?" Asher prompts after several long moments.

"After the battle, if we survive…I don't know." I look up at him. "I don't want to belong to anyone anymore. That's all I know for sure."

"You belong *with* me, not *to* me," Asher says softly. "You could rule by my side, as my equal."

A shiver runs through me as my emotions war with each other. How is it I can feel so many opposing things all at once?

"I'll take that into consideration," I whisper.

"Well," he says with a small smile, "That's a vast improvement over a knife at my throat."

He kisses me once more, this time not gently at all, this time stealing all of my breath, making my heart race and my magic spin. When he finally pulls back, he rolls off the bed and stands in one swift movement.

"For now," he says, "We face *this* day. And this day we go to war."

FORTY-ONE

As the first blush of dawn creeps across the sky, my warriors march from the courtyard of our makeshift home. I do not make a grand speech. We all know what we face. This day is not like the many, many others over the centuries.

Today we face something new and terrible.

There's a part of me that thrills at the knowledge that this weapon, Ellielle's plan, has changed the course of this monotonous war once and for all.

Another part of me is absolutely terrified that I have found Zara, the counterpart to my own magic and soul, only to have her ripped away from me just as quickly. It's beyond ironic that these two things have transpired at the same time. Before, I would gladly have welcomed an honorable death.

But now I have something to live for.

My gelding snorts and prances beneath me, arching his muscular neck to impress Zara's chestnut mare. The mare simply pins her ears and weaves her head at him, teeth bared. She shares the same sentiments as her mistress, it seems. I can't help but smile. Zara shoots me a strange look when she sees my expression.

We travel through back streets, a small group of only a hundred warriors. The banners of House Daemonium carried by the cavalry ripple in the cold morning breeze, a crescent moon aflame with a single star at the apex. Shadows of purple and gray surround us, the sun having barely risen above the horizon and still hidden behind the fog of the Waste. It is hushed, the air taut with tension and purpose. Only the sound of hoofbeats and boots on the cobblestones break the silence.

It takes nearly an hour to reach the river. We stop on the border of Syreni territory which expands about a block away from the river's edge, a thin strip of land along the water. The bridge rises directly ahead of us. I pull my horse to a halt and look left and right until I see my generals move into place a few hundred yards to either side with their own battalions. They signal to me that the other battalions further from the bridge are also in place. Six small groups of us lined up along the riverside, a thousand Daemonium strong in total.

The sun has climbed higher now and there's a fiery smear of orange along the top edges of the Waste, the sky above it a pale dove gray that bleeds into the clouds. Zara pulls the mare alongside my horse, her leg brushing mine, her gaze intent as she stares across into Angelus territory. A ray of sun breaks through the fog, making the mare glow bronze and painting Zara's own dark hair with gold, her eyes also.

I do not know if we will win this battle. I do not know if we will survive this day. But I do know, with more certainty than anything I've ever known in my life, that I will burn this whole city to the ground if it means keeping Zara safe. Nothing is more important to me than the woman riding at my side.

She looks over at me, sensing my gaze, and I reach out and squeeze her fingers once quickly before letting go. Then I turn to look behind me at Marin, the battalion leader of the Incantrix who will help us take the bridge. Marin nods tersely from where she sits astride her black horse. I feel the swell of magic at my back like a brewing storm.

"It's time," I say, my words, while not loud, reverberating down the line of warriors behind me.

I shoot Zara one last look, and then we kick our horses into a gallop and charge the bridge.

When we get within fifty feet, I call the wild magic and send a blast out ahead of us. The Syreni guards scream and duck for cover as the wave of purple light moves toward them. The water of the river, however, is unbroken by the Mer, who are no doubt hiding until all this is over. Zara's mare runs faster and hits the bridge a couple strides before my horse. We gallop across, Marin and the other Incantrix at our heels. I hear the roar of the fire demons as they merge into the stream of warriors making the first charge.

On the other end of the bridge, I can see the glimmer of a thick magical forcefield blocking the entrance into Angelus territory. Dozens of winged warriors flank the bridge, and as we move, I see dozens more arriving, by air and by foot, no doubt signaled by the noise of our arrival. They've clearly been expecting us. Ellielle is no fool.

Zara and I both send blasts of magic toward the forcefield, as do the Incantrix behind us. Dozens of arcs of magic shoot like comets, lighting up the barrier as they make impact. The shield flickers but holds. The bridge shakes as Verok's fire battalion charges up behind us. The demons begin to add their own magic to the siege breaking like a storm on the Angelus border. More and more angels arrive to bolster the forces on their side of the bridge. We'll have to fight through hundreds once we break the barrier, not to mention however many more lie between here and Ellielle's tower.

I rein in my horse as we reach the forcefield. He spins and snorts, eyes wild, chest flecked with foam from the charge. On instinct, I reach out and grab Zara's hand, summoning the wild magic as I do. I feel Zara open herself to it as well, and Night glows and shifts beneath us. The power that moves through us is more intense than anything I've felt before, other than the day I first released the power that doomed this city.

Magic pours out of us like the sun and moon both, like

a thousand storms and a thousand oceans. The forcefield glitters and shatters, blasting all the Angelus off their feet as our pulse of power roils over them.

I drop Zara's hand. She looks over at me, her chest heaving from the intensity of the magic that moved through us. Her eyes still glow, a pale ring of lavender around her darker purple pupils. A shiver moves over me, and it's all I can do not to pull her off her horse and taste the lingering power on her lips.

"Ready?" I ask, nodding toward the masses of angels a dozen paces away. They're beginning to get to their feet, staggering and dazed from what hit them.

She nods, a sharp jerk of her chin.

It's at that moment, as I look back at her, that I see something huge land on top of the building nearest the bridge on the Syreni side. A tremor shakes the bridge as it lands, its massive claws crushing the stone parapet it landed on. Golden wings flare out behind it and it lets out a roar that shakes the entire city.

A dragon shifter.

Not just any dragon shifter, but the Lord of Animus. My brother, Kieran.

More winged beasts land on nearby buildings all along the river. Dragons and gryphons and massive eagles and hawks. And at street level, I see other creatures arriving. Bears, panthers, and wolves. A chorus of magnificent and bone-shattering howls rise up behind us. Then, from the river, dozens upon dozens of Syreni surface in unison, balls of magic at the ready.

The Animus faction has surrounded us from behind. We're now trapped between enemy factions. This can't be a coincidence.

My brother and the Syreni have joined forces with Ellielle.

FORTY-TWO

ZARA

I recognize the dragon that alights on top of the building in an instant. *Kieran.* My heart comes to an abrupt stop as the man I once thought I loved, the man I once devoted all my loyalty to, stares down on me and Asher.

It's clear he's come to kill us.

To kill all of us. Animus, Syreni, and Angelus joined together against the Daemonium. It's an alliance meant for one thing: to annihilate their common enemy.

I wonder, fleetingly, if Kieran would have told me had I not confronted him last night. Or would he have let me walk into this unwittingly, still playing the part he sent me here to play? I've only ever been a pawn to him. Just as Lyri was. Just as we all are.

But none of that matters now. I made my choice and I don't regret it, even if it means my death on this battlefield today.

I turn to Asher. "Ahead," I growl. "We can't stop now."

He nods and we open the horses up again, pressing our heels to their sides, leaping off the bridge and into the throngs of Angelus who are beginning to get back on their feet after our joint magical attack. I can still feel the after-effects of it thrumming within me. I've never felt anything so powerful. Had Asher meant what he said? Would he really rule by my side? After feeling what I just felt when we joined our magic together, intentionally, without the inner battle I'd fought all the times before, it seems there's nothing we can't do.

And for the first time in my life, I feel true hope.

If we can only get to this magical weapon before Ellielle detonates it and causes untold horrors to Night and its people.

Our horses gallop through the fallen angels, Incantrix and Daemonium behind us. We make it about halfway across the large plaza on the other side of the bridge before the Angelus fully recover from our attack and are able to fight back. It's as if we'd been traveling across an open field, only to have a forest suddenly spring up around us.

Angels swarm us, hands and weapons and magic coming at us from every direction. Asher and I immediately go on the defense, blocking spear and sword and bright light that looks almost like lightning bolts. The horses snort and let out shrill cries as our enemies press in around us. After several moments, I stop trying to block and send out another pulse of magic that knocks back those closest to us. Asher does the same and we cut a path through to the other side of the plaza.

"This way!" he calls, jerking the reins of his gelding to steer him down a narrow side street.

We pick up speed, galloping toward Ellielle's tower. A few of the Incantrix make it through and follow as we leave the crush of the battle behind. For several moments, it seems we've made a clean break, but then I sense a shadow overhead and feel the rush of wings.

I duck at the last moment as one of the Angelus swoops down. The blast of magic they threw at me glances off my shoulder instead of hitting the back of my head as intended. Magical fire burns along my skin and a gasp escapes my throat as pain radiates through my body. My vision goes black a moment and I sway in the saddle before righting myself.

Screams ring out behind me as several of the Incantrix take direct hits from other angels, a whole battalion of them converging above us. I want to go back for them, but I know I can't. To stop now means to die, and means that Ellielle will destroy this whole city.

We reach an intersection and gallop across, catching rapid fire from another dozen angels waiting for us on the rooftops. Asher and I each let out blasts of our own magic, managing to reach the other side and dart between buildings again. More cries of agony ring out behind us, and my chest tightens as tears burn in my throat. I've lost many, many comrades in battle. But never before have I been the one to lead them to their deaths.

I can see the tower ahead between the gaps in the buildings. We're drawing close. Asher's horse is a nose ahead, and after we cross the next intersection, he darts into an even narrower passage, an alley. One of the angels tries to follow, but his wingspan is too wide and he ricochets off the walls before plummeting to the ground in a spray of rock dust. The horses keep moving at breakneck speed, Asher's gray gelding in the lead, my chestnut mare on his tail. A glance over my shoulder shows me that two Incantrix are still with us.

The shadows of the angels follow us above the tops of the buildings. Ellielle's tower is just ahead now, and from what Asher has said, the weapon is in the building behind it. Our alleyway is running out fast, the wide expanse of a courtyard ahead. We'll be completely out in the open, completely unprotected. There's not enough room to ride at Asher's side, to touch him so we can join our magic again.

Asher's horse shoots out into the open, and as if sensing my thoughts, he reins him in hard, throwing his arm out to me. My mare springs free of the alleyway and I stretch for his fingers, already summoning my magic, already pouring it outward even as I reach for Asher. Our fingertips brush, and then the chestnut mare screams and flips beneath me.

The world cartwheels. I watch her head and neck catapult toward the cobblestones as I'm launched off her back. See the red spray of her mane, or maybe her blood, as I soar above her. A flash of gray sky. The roil of the

Waste in the distance. The jade green of an angel's wings.

And then black, nothingness, as I collide with the earth at tremendous speed.

Pain is all I know for several moments. I can't see anything. I can't feel my body. My existence is agony.

A brilliant wash of magic moves over me, clears the darkness from my vision.

I force myself up onto my hands and knees. The right side of my body is a bruised and bloody mess. Asher stands a few feet away, raining destruction down on a host of angels. Already, in just a handful of moments, a dozen bodies lie dead around him. His gelding stands over my mare, nose touching her lifeless body, snorting at the sharp scent of blood coming from the silver spear in her chest. One of our Incantrix lies dead a stone's throw behind them.

Rage propels me to my feet. I stagger forward a couple of steps and then I add my magic to Asher's, moving steadily toward him until we can grasp hands. The wave of power that comes next knocks every angel in the courtyard out of the sky.

When the pulse of our magic dissipates, Asher pulls me against him and kisses me fiercely. "If you die, I will destroy *everything*. Do you hear me?" he growls.

My heart flips in my chest, and I nod.

We turn, hands still interlaced, and we run for the building beyond the tower courtyard.

We make it to an arched stone entryway, where Asher

points toward a church on the far side of a smaller court-yard. A quick glance around shows no defense here, other than two guards at the door. I'm guessing there are quite a few more inside.

"What's the plan when we're inside?" I ask Asher, looking up at him. "How do we disable this thing without unleashing all the trapped magic?"

"We break it. Then we absorb all of the excess magic, together." His eyes burn into mine and his jaw rolls. "And we pray that we can do that without dire consequences to Night."

It's not reassuring, but I'd known that before I asked. So, I simply nod, and we stride for the doorway behind which the fate of the world lies.

As we approach, I raise my hand to blast the guards out of the way. But before I can release my magic, a figure appears out of nothing on the roof of the church. A cloaked figure who jumps down and cuts the throat of each guard in the blink of an eye.

The bodies fall limp at his feet and Falling Star turns to face us.

"Stop where you are," Falling Star calls, raising a hand in warning. "I'm only going to ask you once."

Asher lets out a low growl and magic pulses through him, but I grab his arm. "No!"

He shoots me a confused look, and I realize I can't myself explain why I want to protect the leader of the Factionless rebels. I tear my gaze from Asher and pin it on Falling Star.

"We don't want to hurt you," I say. "But we have to disable the weapon. If that thing goes off, it's going to cause catastrophic damage."

Falling Star cocks his head to the side. "And the answer is you two taking the power?" He snorts. "You already have more than enough. You're far more dangerous than that thing inside."

"No." I shake my head. "We're not. Because we can control that much wild magic. But without a conduit? Night would be destroyed."

"A convenient story woven by those who wish to maintain control." Falling Star shakes his head. "I confess, Zara, I am disappointed to see you with *him* again." A jerk of the chin toward Asher.

I still can't see Falling Star's face, but I can sense the intense emotion pouring off of him. A shiver and a spike of unease move through me. "And why do you care so much about the actions of a stranger?"

"Enough of this," Asher snarls, raising his arm toward Falling Star.

Asher's magic pulses at the same moment that Falling Star pulls back the hood of his cloak and drops his shadow spell.

I have just the merest fraction of a moment to slam my body into Asher's so his shot flies wide.

Because the person standing uncloaked before me isn't a stranger at all. And it's also not a man. It's a woman with long black hair tied in a braid framing tawny cheeks, her purple eyes burning into me. I could be staring into a mirror because she looks just like me.

"Jaylen," I gasp, hope and shock and anguish twisting around my heart like barbed wire.

My sister, who is very much not dead, stares back at me.

And it's in that moment the building behind us explodes in a firestorm of wild magic.

CHAPTER
FORTY-THREE
ASHER

The world does not exist for several long heartbeats, or perhaps an eternity.

I don't know how much times passes. All I know is the storm of wild magic that consumes everything. It rips through me, it tears me apart, it puts me back together again. Infinite and endless and ending, all at once.

And then there is silence.

My eyes blink open and I realize I am still alive. I still possess a body. The magic has not consumed me after all.

Sensation returns to me slowly. I'm lying on my back, the stone rough against my skin. Dust fills the air, and it contains a purple glow from the magic still hanging thick around me. But dust from what? Panic churns in my stomach.

Where is Zara?

I flip over, head spinning as I scan the courtyard. I still

can't hear anything. The blast must have damaged my hearing. It's too unnaturally quiet.

She's not next to me where she had been. She's not behind me, either. As terror spikes through me, my eyes finally land on her through the strange, pulsating air: she's lying by the cloaked woman, shielding her with her body. They're both intact, and I see Zara stir. She's alive. As is the other woman, the one she'd called Jaylen…

Zara's sister.

But all thoughts of her sister and how she came to be here fly from my head when I see what lies beyond the two women.

For a moment I wonder if I'm hallucinating. I struggle to sit up, wiping my eyes as I do. The source of the dust becomes abruptly clear. Because the church that housed the weapon is nothing but a pile of rubble. And not just that one, but every building beyond it, a swath of destruction about twenty feet wide that continues north. It's as if the wild magic bounced off of me and Zara and shot the other direction, cutting like a laser across the city.

Not just the city.

My heart stops beating in my chest.

Because the line cut by the blast of wild magic doesn't stop at the Waste. It cuts right through it, creating a path as far as the eye can see. The gray fog roils on either side of it. I expect it to drift back in to fill the void, but it stays where it is as if held in place by an invisible wall.

I shove myself up onto my hands and knees, and then

upright. Staggering, I take a step toward Zara, then another step. When I reach her, I fall to my knees again, hands hovering over her, fingers trembling.

"Zara?"

She stirs and opens her eyes, letting out a groan and clutching her ribcage. Jaylen doesn't move, but I can see her chest rising and falling as she breathes, though it's halting and hitched.

"Can you hear me?"

Zara nods.

I slide one hand under the back of her head. "Can you sit up?"

Another nod.

Slowly, I help her into an upright position. She looks down at her sister and lets out an anguished cry.

"She's alive. Be still," I command.

She nods, panning her gaze slowly around us. She freezes when she sees the rift across Night. "What in the dark goddess..."

"We'll worry about that later." I pull her gently against me. "You're alive, and that's all that matters to me."

Zara's eyes meet mine, and I bend and kiss her. I don't know where Ellielle is, or if the battle still wages by the river. And I can't even fathom what this rift has done to Night and the Waste and what to do about that. Right now, we just need to get to safety.

Zara clings to me as I help her to her feet. Her face and hair are covered in dust, and blood streaks her cheek.

"I—I can't feel my magic," she whispers against me, her words vibrating my chest.

With a pulse of shock, I realize I can't feel mine, either. I hadn't even noticed in the chaos. "We'll figure that out later. We'll figure everything out later."

I bend and kiss her again, and the heat that moves between us this time has nothing to do with magic or power or Night. Zara kisses me back like she wants me just as much. Like maybe, just maybe, one day she could come to feel the way about me that I feel about her.

"Asher," she says breathlessly, pulling back. "I want to—"

But I don't get a chance to hear what she wants to say, because a voice cuts through the swirling dust, followed a moment later by a tall figure making his way toward us.

"Falling in love with my brother was never part of the plan, Zara."

Kieran stops a dozen feet away. He's back in human form, dirty and bloody but otherwise uninjured from the battle. Confusion worms through my brain as I watch his eyes cut to Zara's. She tenses against me.

I shake my head. "What?"

"The *plan,*" Kieran says, a small smile on his lips. "*My* plan. For Zara. Surely, now that you two are so close, she told you?"

Zara looks up at me, face stricken, purple eyes wide.

"What is he talking about?" I ask, meeting those imploring eyes, a roil of nausea stabbing through my gut.

"Asher," she begins, "It only started that way—"

"*Ahh*. So, she didn't tell you." Kieran crosses his arms over his chest, his smile twisting into a cruel smirk. "Zara is *mine*. She's Animus. She always has been."

The world spins a second time.

"**I** am *not* yours," I hiss, glaring at Kieran. "I made it very clear I no longer work for you."

I can feel the thrum of Asher's heart against my collarbone from where I'm huddled in the circle of his arms. His whole body is rigid like bands of iron.

"You've been working for my brother? This whole time?" His face goes from blank surprise to ice-cold anger, a growl entering his voice.

"Not the whole time." I shake my head. "At first, yes. But then things changed."

I stare up at him, pivoting so he can see my eyes, so he can see I'm telling the truth. I slide my hand over his heart.

"So, you came to work for me, get close to me, all because of him?" Asher's eyes flash with fury and he jerks his head toward Kieran.

"No, not entirely—" I begin.

"She wanted to kill you," Kieran says with a sharp

laugh. "I told her she'd have to spy on you first. That didn't make her happy... an impatient one, my shadow witch."

"You know why," I say. My voice sounds pleading, desperate, but I don't care. "I told you the truth about that."

I point to the ground where Jaylen had been lying, but she's not there. Panic spikes through my veins. She must have crawled away while we were distracted by Kieran. I can't lose her again, not after finally finding her.

Asher steps away from me, his eyes more dangerous and deadly than I've ever seen them. "I could have endured the fact that you wanted me dead. At least I understand why."

His eyes cut to Kieran, and the burn of hatred grows a thousand-fold.

"But working for my brother... belonging to my *brother*..."

"Asher, please," I beg, stepping toward him again.

He shoves me away from him, hard. I fall backward onto the cobblestones at Kieran's feet.

"Anything else, Zara," he says, his voice soft but carrying so much power it makes me tremble. "Anything else in all the world I would endure for you. But not this. Not *him*."

"Do not feel foolish, brother," Kieran says. "She made me think she loved me, too." He shakes his head. "It took me too long to realize that all she seeks is power."

"Take her, then," Asher says. His eyes on mine are

devoid of emotion now, the mask of the Lord of Night firmly in place. "It seems she belongs rightfully to you. I don't *ever* want to see her again."

And I realize, then, as my heart ices over and goes still in my chest, that the only person I've been truly lying to this whole time is myself. I'd told Asher as we lay in bed that I didn't know what I wanted. But now, feeling him withdraw from me, feeling his icy hatred, it's clear from the agony that rips through my core that I've been deceiving myself most of all.

The sound of marching footsteps coming up behind us sends my gaze spinning over my shoulder. Two dozen warriors, Animus and Angelus both, move across the remains of the courtyard to flank us. In the distance, I see Ellielle watching, gray wings tucked behind her, black hair blowing in the breeze.

I climb to my feet in a hurry, but without my magic I have little defense against numbers this great.

"Take her," Kieran says to the Animus that approach, pointing at me. "Ellielle will deal with the former Lord of Night."

"Asher, don't do this," I say, trying to meet his gaze.

"I'm not the one who did this," he says as the Animus flank me, grabbing me by the elbows.

"I do *not* belong to you!" I snarl at Kieran, but he only smiles. I struggle against my captors, but I have no strength after the blast. "Asher!" I scream as they drag me away. "Asher!"

My second scream is drowned out, however, by a

much larger sound. The blast of something, a blast like a thousand horns of war blown in the same instant, deep and resonant as it booms across the land. A sound that came from…

All heads spin toward the Waste.

There, far in the distance, something can be seen. Something traveling down the rift created by the explosion of wild magic.

Something coming for Night.

Subscribe to Aurora's Newsletter at
https://bit.ly/3tLmnfi

Subscribers receive an exclusive extra City of Night scene
not available anywhere else - plus book giveaways,
advance reading copies, and ALL the latest news!

WANT TO BE AN
AUTHOR'S BEST FRIEND?

Blood, sweat, tears, wine, and a little piece of my soul went into writing this book. I'd love to know what you think! Leave a review on Goodreads and your book retailer of choice. Tell me your favorite character or your favorite scene. Reviews help authors a ton, both in ranking algorithms and making a living, so I much appreciate it!

You can also email me a note or send fan art (I LOVE fan art!) to auroragreyauthor@gmail.com

And come chat with me on Facebook, Instagram, TikTok, or BookBub!

ABOUT THE AUTHOR

 Aurora Grey lives in Florida with her dog, too many cats, and a very mischievous horse. She writes stories about magic, swoonworthy dudes, and the strong, sexy women they fall for. When not enjoying books, she can be found traveling, a glass of champagne in hand.

Keep up with ALL the latest news! Sign up for Aurora's newsletter on her website:
www.AuroraGreyAuthor.com

She also likes to hang on:
Instagram: instagram.com/auroragreyauthor
TikTok: tiktok.com/@auroragreyauthor
Facebook: facebook.com/auroragreyauthor
BookBub: bookbub.com/authors/aurora-grey

Printed in Great Britain
by Amazon

42551482R00179